Sarah Jules

*Cover by Christy Aldridge at Grim Poppy Design*

*Proofread by Mary Hoyle*

*Published by Mark of the Witch Press*

*For the good boys and girls who fight our demons every day.*

*Author note: This book is written in British English. Therefore, dear American readers, there may be a few less z's than you're anticipating. Us Brits also spell some words differently too, don't worry about it. These aren't typos, I promise. <3*

Contents

# Psychic Cleansing Services

by Lilith Lavelle

IS SOMETHING HAPPENING IN YOUR HOME, AND YOU DON'T KNOW WHAT?

ARE YOU SEEING SHADOWS, HEARING VOICES, EXPERIENCING MOVING OBJECTS?

MAYBE THE ENERGY IN YOUR HOME JUST FEELS 'OFF'.

YOU DON'T HAVE TO SUFFER IN SILENCE.

GET IN TOUCH FOR A NO-OBLIGATION QUOTE.

100% GUARANTEED SUCCESS!

SPECIALISING IN:

- Poltergeist Activity
- Demonic Activity
- Energy Imbalances
- Residual Hauntings
- Shadow People

# Preying on Innocents

The tension headache that had pulsed behind Felix's right eye for the entirety of the last term had finally dissipated. For the first time in weeks, he could relax. The sun was out, the grass was green, and there were no angsty teenagers within twenty feet of him. Perfection. As much as he loved his job, he spent an inordinate amount of time trying to convince teenagers, who were too focused on their social lives, anxiety, and hormones, that Shakespeare was still relevant, even if he didn't entirely believe it was true himself. Now that the college kids he lectured were free to be left to their own devices, he had a full six weeks of quality time with his son, Asher, ahead of him. And he planned to make the most of it.

'Here,' Eli said, handing Felix a paper cup filled with black coffee. Felix's brother's eyes scanned the park for Asher and Specs. He paused, and then waved his free hand in the air. A huge smile tore across Asher's face as he spotted his uncle before he went back to throwing the ball for Specs. Specs, Eli's dopey rescue dog, only had eyes for Asher. Specs followed Asher's every command, and never so much as even looked at another living soul when Asher was there, which made taking them to the park a fairly relaxing experience for all involved.

'Isn't Specs tired yet?' Eli asked. The queue for the coffee had trailed outside of the café. Eli had been gone for at least twenty minutes, in which time Asher had continuously thrown the ball for Specs, who dropped it at his feet, tail thumping on the ground, over and over again, eager for Asher to continue their game.

'Apparently not.' Felix found himself smiling. Specs had been a godsend for Asher. The two of them were the best of friends. Ten years ago, when Eli brought this slobbery mess of a puppy home, with too-big paws and a Staffy grin that would rival the Joker's smile, Felix had been sceptical. But Specs proved him wrong at every juncture. Specs was nothing but gentle with Asher, even though the kid had been barely two years old at the time.

Eli sat on the bench beside Felix, pulled out his phone, and took a photo of Specs and Asher. Felix glanced over at his brother. Eli was, objectively, the better looking of the two of them. While Felix was the lanky kid with long limbs that he never quite grew into, Eli was tall but broad. Perfectly proportioned. Eli was the light to Felix's dark. The blonde hair, to Felix's muddy brown hair. The blue eyes to Felix's… also muddy brown.

'Shit, I forgot, I have something to show you.' Eli scrolled through the photos on his phone and then thrust it at Felix.

The screenshot was of a, very poorly done, advert for *psychic cleansing services.* Whatever that was supposed to be.

Felix scanned the advert, failing to prevent his eyes from rolling.

'Poltergeist activity? Residual hauntings? Shadow people? How the fuck can she guarantee 100% success on something that doesn't actually exist?' Felix shook his head, studying the advert further.

'Because she can be sure as shit the poltergeist isn't in the house. It never existed. Success guaranteed.' Eli laughed, shaking his head at the idiocy of the whole thing.

'Fuck,' Felix said. 'How does she get away with that?'

'What, like there's an OFSTED for psychics?' Eli said, taking a sip of his latte.

'There should be. It's fraud. She's offering a service to get rid of something that doesn't exist to begin with.'

'One that people are willing to pay for. It's their money. Some people have more money than sense.' Eli's eyebrows furrowed. A questioning expression painted his face, one Felix hadn't seen since the wake of Jenna's death.

'I thought you'd find it funny,' he said.

'You thought wrong,' Felix snapped, instantly regretting it. 'Sorry.'

He inhaled through his nose, held it a beat, and released it through his mouth. A technique one of the NHS mental health practitioners had taught him after Jenna's car accident. It got Felix through some difficult moments back then. He was painfully aware that the practitioner would have encouraged him to figure out why his reaction to this Lilith character was so visceral. Anger felt like a living creature under his skin. He was overwhelmed by the intense desire to know more about Lilith Lavelle's psychic scam.

'This is fucked up, Eli,' Felix said. He re-read the advert. 'She's preying on innocent people.'

'Which is what snake oil salesmen do,' Eli agreed. 'It's messed up, but it's their money. If it makes them feel better, let them get on with it.'

'You know as well as I do that this is bullshit.'

'I do, but what can you do?' Eli shrugged like this didn't impact him at all.

Felix handed Eli back the phone. He pulled his own phone from his pocket and opened Google, searching '*Lilith Lavelle*'. Her website was the first link, followed by her Instagram, Facebook, and LinkedIn. He clicked on her website with shaking fingers.

'What're you doing?' Eli asked, peering over the phone.

Felix couldn't tear his eyes away from the screen.

'Look at this.' Felix passed his phone to Eli. Pins and needles of rage prickled at his skin. On her webpage was a review from a woman called Carol. Based on her name, and the nature of the review, he assumed that she was elderly, or at least knocking on a bit. Lilith had down-right fucked her over.

*Lilith Lavelle was a saint. After my son, Tristan, died after a long battle with cancer, he was trapped in our realm and couldn't move on to the other side. I could feel his presence in the house. How he was in pain and ached to be on the other side where he belonged. I called Lilith after one of my friends had success with her, and she came the next day. By the end of that day, Tristan passed into the light. I wouldn't have believed it, if I hadn't seen it myself. I've never believed in ghosts or trapped spirits, but she helped my baby pass over and I am so incredibly grateful to her. When Tristan passed over, the energy of the house completely changed and I could no longer feel his presence there. I am able to rest easily now knowing that Tristan is where he is safe, and happy. I would highly recommend Lilith's services to anybody whose loved one is stuck after their death, and who wants to help them move on to a better place.*

*Value for money:* ★★★★★

*Refer to a friend:* ★★★★★

*Quality of service:* ★★★★★

*Overall:* ★★★★★

'Fuck.' Eli exhaled, shaking his head. 'That's rough.'

'How does she live with herself?' Felix couldn't wrap his head around what kind of a person could prey on grieving people like that. Carol was one of many reviews filling Lilith's page. She made her living by ripping off people when they were at their worst and most vulnerable.

'Have you seen Lilith's comment?' Eli said, tentatively handing back the phone.

*It was a pleasure to help your son pass into the light. Thank you for the awesome review!*

'This is fucking insane. There's no light. You know there's no fucking light.' Felix's face grew warm in frustration. He'd been the same since he was a kid, unable to hide his feelings because they plastered themselves as plain as day on his face.

'Shhh.' Eli placed his hand on Felix's shoulder. People were glancing their way. Felix bowed his head, sheepishly. There was no light, he knew that better than anybody. When a loved one died, they faded away into what their mum called 'the beyond', sometimes they hung around for a while first, but they would always vanish eventually. The *light* was nothing more than a myth. The first time he'd watched a spirit decide that enough was enough and they didn't want to be here anymore, he didn't have a clue what was happening. The core memory was tattooed indelibly into his memory, he could still see his mum's smiling face in front of five-year-old Felix.

'You can see them too?' she'd said.

He'd nodded, crying into her soft chest. She held him tight and told him there was nothing to be scared of; that these were people, just like him, but they had passed away. They were as natural as anything else. Except, not everybody had the gift to see them. It was a gift his mum took seriously.

Grief was the most powerful emotion and to take advantage of a grieving parent, saying that you helped their son to pass on into a light that didn't exist, was the lowest of the low.

'Is this about Jenna? I shouldn't have shown it to you. I didn't think.'

'Jenna has nothing to do with this,' Felix said through gritted teeth. Blood rushed to his temples, and his headache reinvigorated. He felt like he might collapse at any moment.

# Late Night Doom Scrolling

If Felix listened carefully, he could hear Asher's gentle snores creeping through the floorboards. The soothing noise was the signal he'd been waiting for. What he was about to do felt dirty; sickening. He didn't know why, but the last thing he wanted was for Asher to know about his new obsession. *Lilith Lavelle.* The woman who pounced on those who were at their most vulnerable and used them to pay her bills. He'd been dying to jump down the rabbit hole all day, but knowing how it had affected him when Eli first shared her page, he didn't want Asher to see him like that. That was parenting 101: don't let your kid see you break down.

Felix switched on Netflix on the TV and clicked on a series he had no interest in watching. Cast in the blue glow of the screen, he searched her name on Google from his phone. He bypassed the website, choosing to focus on her social media. Her Instagram was the first one to pop up. He wasn't sure what he expected, but he was still caught off guard. Lilith's face beamed at him from most of the tiles, her arm around different *clients* of hers. Her blonde hair fell to her waist in loose curls, reminding him of Rapunzel. She wore workout clothes, tight leggings and oversized jumpers, not exactly what you'd expect from a *professional psychic cleanser*. The usual psychic types were goths, dyed black hair, and eyeliner that winged outward. Or, alternatively, they were middle-aged dumpy women, desperate to make a quick buck. These were the kinds you'd find at fairgrounds attempting to lure you into their caravan. Lilith was, well, *lighter?* More *normal?* Felix wasn't sure those were the right words, but they were what came to mind. The clients all wore smiles that rivalled Lilith's. They believed that she'd, somehow, magically fixed their lives by banishing their poltergeists, sending their loved ones to the other side, or whatever else she'd claimed to be able to do.

The more he scrolled, the more annoyed he became. Any sane person would have put the phone down and done something else. Felix? No. He scrolled and scrolled, each one of the smiling clients felt like a knife in his side. Twisting and burning.

How many of them had just lost loved ones?

How many of them were suffering from mental health issues?

How many were just plain terrified?

And there went Lilith Lavelle to save the day, offering her magical (and completely unsubstantiated) services for a presumably extortionate fee. He'd wager that all she did was burn some sage and say some kind of nonsense *spell*. She'd have to make it a little theatrical for people to believe her, which only bittered the taste in his mouth further.

There was one photograph that grabbed him by the throat and wouldn't let go. A young family; mum, dad, and baby. By their side stood Lilith Lavelle, staring directly at him through the screen. The caption read: *'So #thankful to support the Smith family with the passing of their daughter, Samantha.'* He scrolled right and found a photograph of a family of four, the Smiths and what was presumably their daughter Samantha in a hospital bed. The girl looked to be maybe three or four years old; the baby in the mother's arms looked only a few months younger than they did in the first photo. Samantha was ravaged by some unknown illness. His brain flashed with the C-word. CANCER CANCER CANCER. That was the only thing that he knew could make children look like that. Hollowed cheekbones, no hair, a painful smile.

Beneath was a comment from the mother. 'Thank you so much for helping my little girl.'

Felix swallowed the bile that burned at his throat.

*Click here to read the full story.*

He did. He shouldn't have. The link took him to her website.

*When Johnny and Emily Smith reached out to me, they had just lost their beloved daughter, Samantha, to leukaemia a week before. Samantha died in the hospital following a short, but very brave, battle with this horrible disease. Her parents were obviously beside themselves with their loss. They had a quiet funeral service for close friends and family and Samantha's body was cremated. However, when they returned home from the funeral they began to hear Samantha's laugh, her footsteps running down the hall, her breathing when they slept. They knew that Samantha's spirit hadn't moved on. They reached out to me via direct message and I visited with them the next day. When I walked into their home, I immediately felt Samantha's presence. The poor thing was stuck there. After spending a short while tuning into Samantha's energy, I could tell that she was scared to leave her parents, and her little brother, alone because they were all so sad that she'd died. She was frustrated that they couldn't see her and that they were ignoring her. Of course, this wasn't intentional. Together with her parents, we explained to Samantha what had happened to her and were able to convince her to move on. This world is not meant for the dead, they have to slip beyond the veil by walking into the light. It took a little convincing, and a lot of tears, but eventually Samantha walked into the light and her parents knew that she was safe and sound, and where she was meant to be. They were therefore then able to start their grieving process.*

*To get in touch, direct message or reach out via my website!*

Felix couldn't even begin to imagine the pain of losing a child. Especially to something as insidious as cancer. He remembered in the days and weeks that followed Jenna's death, he'd think that he saw her so often. He'd catch a glimpse of somebody who looked vaguely similar and, for a split second, would believe with his whole heart that it was his wife. Of course, it wasn't. He'd never seen Jenna's spirit, not once, since her death. He saw spirits all the time, it wasn't until his early teens that he'd learned to distinguish the living from the dead. He was now able to adeptly ignore their presence. But he'd never seen Jenna. It made sense to Felix that in the days after Samantha's death, her parents would believe that they could hear her in their home. Surely that was a normal part of the grieving process, and for Lilith to take advantage of that… he couldn't find the words to say how that made him feel. The woman was sick. Twisted. She needed to be stopped.

Already on her website, he found the 'contact me' page and began to fill in the form.

Name, email address, query. He'd begun to fill it out before he could change his mind, determined to prove that Lilith Lavelle was scamming people during the worst times of their lives. He couldn't allow it to continue.

*Dear Ms Lavelle*

*I'm hoping you might be able to help me. I've been experiencing something strange in my home and I need your help. It started a couple of weeks ago. I began hearing strange voices speaking in another language. I couldn't make out what they were saying. Then cold spots began to develop in my house. I'd walk through them and immediately feel frozen to my core. The worst of it has been the shadow figures. At first, I only saw them out of the corner of my eye. Then it progressed. I began to see them when the lights were dimmed standing in the corners of my room. I don't know what to do. I'm scared for my son's safety. I need your help.*

*Yours sincerely,*

*Felix Eastwood*

After he pressed send, he closed his eyes and tipped his head back. He wouldn't allow himself to question if he'd done the right thing or not. The Smiths, and so many other families, had been duped into thinking that Lilith Lavelle had saved their loved ones. Taking advantage of somebody who had lost a loved one was one thing, but taking advantage of families who had lost children was the lowest of the low, as far as Felix was concerned.

Something tugged in his chest. Asher. Felix needed to be near him. Asher was at that funny age where he was more than happy to cuddle at home, but would stand at least two feet away from Felix when they were out of the house. Sometimes he still crawled into Felix's bed after having a nightmare, not as often as he used to, but part of Felix (a larger part than he cared to admit) loved it when Asher slept next to him. Ever since Jenna's death, his son was the only person to have slept beside him. For better or for worse, that was the case.

Felix climbed the stairs slowly, avoiding the step that creaked, and opened the door to Asher's room. The gentle snores came louder. His heart swelled with pride. The thought of what the Smith family must have gone through with Samantha felt like a vice grip around his chest. Asher was his entire life. If anything happened to him, Felix would have no reason to be here. Standing there, watching his son's chest rise and fall, he knew that he'd done the right thing. He had to stop Lilith Lavelle from exploiting people who were experiencing the worst life had to throw at them.

# Taking the Bait

Felix's eyelids fluttered closed. The summer weather had vanished. Typical British weather. Rain thundered overhead, not quite drowning out the sound of the film Asher had chosen. After being cooped up inside all day, Specs was demanding attention from anybody who would provide it. He paced between Eli and Asher, alternating for belly scratches. The dog knew better than to try Felix, given that he was already on the cusp of sleep.

The vibrations from his pocket startled Felix awake with a snort. Both Asher and Eli turned to face him with wide smiles.

'What was that noise?' Asher teased.

'You're one to talk.' Felix winked at his son. 'You sound like a lawnmower when you're asleep.'

'Hey. That's not true. Right, Uncle Eli?' Asher turned to his uncle with pleading eyes.

'Sorry, kid. You do snore pretty bad.'

The phone continued to buzz in Felix's pocket. He pulled it out and unlocked it. It was a number he didn't recognise. He shrugged and pressed to accept the call.

'Hello.'

'Hello, is that Mr Eastwood?' The voice on the other end of the line was sickeningly sweet, reminding him of Dolores Umbridge from the *Harry Potter* films Asher loved so much.

'Yes, speaking,' he said.

'Oh, great. It's Lilith Lavelle, you got in touch regarding some supernatural activity on your property.'

'Yes, one second,' Felix stuttered.

'No problem,' Lilith said.

He peeled himself out of Eli's too-low sofa and walked into the kitchen.

Felix shut the kitchen door behind him, separating himself from Eli and Asher.

'Thank you for calling me,' Felix said.

'Thank you for getting in touch. I have to admit, I'm very concerned based on what you said in your message. It sounds like whatever energy is present in your home is growing in power. I believe it would be sensible to nip it in the bud, especially if you have a child there with you. May I ask how old your son is?'

'Yes, Asher is twelve.'

'And how is he reacting to the hauntings?'

'Exactly as you would expect,' Felix said. He had no idea how a child would typically react to a haunting. He'd only ever seen it in horror films because, as far as he was concerned, hauntings, in the painfully stereotypical sense that he'd described to Lilith, didn't happen. Ghosts, or spirits as his mother preferred to call them, were just dead energy waiting to move on into the next realm. They often took the form of their earthly bodies because that was all they had known. There was nothing sinister or scary about spirits.

'Of course. I have a space in my diary the day after tomorrow, that would be Tuesday. Would that work for you? The sooner the better, and you can get back to normal again.'

'That would be brilliant, thank you.' Felix said. It struck him immediately that Lilith had space so soon, which likely meant that she wasn't as in demand as her social media presence might otherwise suggest.

'And, just so you're aware, I do charge on a day-by-day basis. Hopefully, one day will be enough to resolve the issue, but just to let you know sometimes it can take two or three days to get these things squared away.'

'Sure,' Felix said. 'And what did you say your day rate was?' He was well aware she hadn't said her day rate, but didn't want to get off on the wrong foot. He needed Lilith to believe this was real, so that she'd treat him exactly like her other clients, or it wouldn't work.

'It's £1250 per day, and that includes any items that I will use in the process.'

It took everything within him to keep the *what the fuck* inside his mouth. For the first time, he began to second guess whether this was worth it. He was on a teacher's salary. Granted, he was on the upper pay scale, but this would take a considerable chunk out of his savings.

'That's fine,' he said, screwing his eyes up as though to absorb the blow. If he could prove Lilith to be a fraud, and stop other desperate people from being taken in by her schemes, then it would be worth it.

He gave his address, and they arranged the time for Lilith to arrive at the house on Tuesday morning (10.30 am, so not even a full day for £1250, he noted).

'I look forward to helping you and your family,' Lilith said as she hung up the phone.

Felix placed the phone on the dining table and raked his hands through his hair. Shit just got real.

'Who was that?' Eli said, pushing the door open and snaking his head through the slit.

'Come here,' Felix said. Eli did as he was asked, shutting the door behind him. 'That was Lilith Lavelle.'

'What the fuck?' Eli whispered. The expression on his face was a strange mixture of confusion and concern.

'I messaged her last night.'

'And why the fuck would you do that?' Eli shook his head, leaning against the kitchen counter.

'Because I can't let her do this to others, Eli. I can't.'

'I knew I shouldn't have… Jesus Christ.' Eli rolled his eyes, placing his hands on his hips. He looked startlingly like their mum.

'She's coming round on Tuesday.'

'Why?' Eli tilted his head, his expression overflowing with reproach.

'Because I told her my house was haunted.'

'Of course you fucking did.' He threw up his hands in a gesture that read '*I give up.*'

Eli turned his back to Felix, resting his elbows on the countertop. He perched his face on top of his open palms.

'You're going to let her in your house?' he mumbled.

'If I can prove she's a fraud, nobody else will fall for it. She won't be able to take advantage of anybody again. I just need her to come here so I can see what she does, and then I can report her, or out her, or something.'

'Why you, Felix? Why do you have to be the one? Why can't you let somebody else do it?'

'Because nobody else has done it, Eli. Have they?' Felix snapped.

'So? This isn't your fight. It isn't. This is a trauma response to Jenna. This isn't about Lilith, and you know it.'

'Don't. Don't do that. It's not about Jenna,' Felix warned.

'Felix, it is. Of course it is. I can't even blame you for that. Jenna's death,' Eli sighed, 'it threw us all. But this isn't anything to do with you.'

'Innocent, desperate people are paying her a fortune to come and help their loved ones walk into the light. The light that doesn't exist. They're at their rock bottom, and she's fucking with them. Do you know how much it costs? Over a grand a day. And she does nothing. These are people who have lost children, Eli. *Children.* She needs to be stopped.'

'So ring the police or something. That's what a normal person would do.'

'And what will they do? They'll say that it's up to the families what they spend their own money on. And I haven't seen what she does yet. I have to be a client, or a customer, or whatever, and then I can report it. Nobody will take me seriously if I haven't used her services.'

'It *is* up to families what they spend their own money on. If it makes them feel better, then what's the harm?' Eli spun around to face Felix.

'I'm going to pretend you didn't just say that.' Felix balled his hands into fists. He hadn't punched his brother since they were kids fighting over who got the best bit of Lego, but the urge to thrust his fist directly into Eli's face was almost overwhelming.

'Fine. Whatever. Do what you want to do. You're an adult. I can't stop you.'

'No, you can't.' Felix, childishly he knew, wanted to have the last word.

'What are you going to tell Asher?'

'The truth. He needs to know the truth.'

As much as it pained Felix, his son would have to be in on the ruse for it to work.

# A Stereotypical Haunting: Part One

When Dad asked him to sit at the kitchen table, Asher knew that something was wrong. He was being treated like a grown-up, and that was never a good thing. They'd spent the whole day at Uncle Eli's and Dad had been in a bad mood. Asher had tried to ignore it, but it had been difficult. At least Specs was in a good mood, as always.

Uncle Eli stayed in the living room with Specs when his dad called him over to the table. He sat down and looked up at his dad, trying to figure out what was wrong.

'I have to talk to you about something,' Dad said.

'Okay,' Asher said.

'There will be a lady coming to the house on Tuesday.'

Asher knew it would happen eventually. That his dad would start dating, but Asher had held out hope that he'd wait until he moved to university to do that. The thought of his dad having *sex* with somebody made him squirm inside. That wasn't what dads were supposed to do.

Asher stayed silent. He didn't want to encourage that kind of behaviour.

'You know about my little gift,' Dad said.

*Little Gift* was what Dad called his ability to see spirits. Gram could do it too, but Uncle Eli and Asher couldn't. Which sucked, because Asher would have loved to see ghosts. It would be awesome, maybe a little scary, but mostly awesome.

'Yes,' Asher said, unsure of where his dad was going. Surely, he couldn't date a ghost. There had to be some law against that.

'Right, so, this lady isn't a good person. She pretends to help people and takes their money. She takes advantage of people who are scared, or poorly, or who have lost people they love. She says that she can help people's loved ones go into the light.'

'But there is no light,' Asher said.

'Right. We know that, but other people don't. They think that their loved ones are trapped here and that they need Lilith Lavelle, that's her name, to help them go to the other side. She also pretends that she can get rid of evil spirits too, like demons and poltergeists. Have you heard of those?'

'Yes, Dad,' Asher said. He might only be twelve, but he wasn't stupid. He played video games, and watched scary movies. Plus, he loved the Goosebumps books, and they were *really* scary.

'So I invited her to our house. I told her that we were being haunted so we can prove that she's lying. If people know she's lying, then they won't give her their money. Does that make sense?'

'Yeah, suppose so,' Asher said.

'We need to make her think that we're being haunted so that we can expose her as a fraud.'

Asher nodded, and then paused to think. 'Couldn't you just tell people that she was lying without doing this?'

'They wouldn't believe us. We have to *prove* it.'

That seemed fair enough to Asher. 'How?'

'We make her believe that our house is haunted by telling her stories.'

'Just stories?' Asher said.

'Yes, just stories.'

'That will work? She'll believe us?'

'It doesn't matter if she believes us. Chances are, she doesn't believe in paranormal stuff anyway, or she wouldn't be in her job, would she?'

Asher considered this for a moment before nodding.

'We need to come up with a story to tell her, so that we're both telling her the same things, okay?'

'Okay,' Asher nodded.

'You don't have to remember everything perfectly. If you're not sure, you can make stuff up. It's not the end of the world.'

Dad pulled out his phone. Asher peered over and watched as his dad opened up the notes app.

'This is what I have so far,' he said. 'We'll tell her that there's a cold spot at the top of the stairs. That means that when you walk up the stairs and onto the landing, you'll feel really really cold. And it's only in that one spot, okay? Nowhere else.'

Asher nodded his head again.

'Okay, next, we've both seen a shadowy figure all around the house, especially at night.'

Asher nodded again.

'And, we'll say that we heard voices, but we can't tell what they're saying. They're muffled, like whispers.'

Asher's dad stopped and thought for a second before typing something into the phone.

'We hear these voices in our bedrooms, when we're going to sleep.'

*Cold spots. Shadowy figures. Voices in bedrooms.* Asher checked that he remembered everything his dad told him.

'Okay,' Asher said. He was beginning to worry that he might not be able to remember everything. He was the top in his class (okay, the second top in his class) but this wasn't exactly typical for a kid his age to do.

'And bumps in the night, and the TV switching itself on and off.'

'Bumps in the night and the TV,' Asher repeated.

'Your toys moving around on their own.'

*Jeez,* Asher thought. But, instead of saying it aloud, he just nodded.

'Got all that?'

'Yeah, I think so.'

'Can you repeat it back to me?'

'Cold spot, shadowy figures, voices in the bedroom, bumps in the night, toys moving. And,' Asher paused, racking his brain, knowing he was missing one thing. 'Oh, and the TV.'

'Good lad,' his dad said. The wide smile told Asher he'd done a good job.

The kitchen door swung open and Uncle Eli stood there, leaning against the door jamb. He shook his head and rolled his eyes at Dad, like they did when they argued. They argued a lot, apparently that's what siblings did, but Asher didn't have any siblings, so he didn't know whether that was true or not.

'I'm having nothing to do with this,' Uncle Eli said.

'Fine. But you won't tell Mum?' Felix said.

'Of course not. Somehow it would be my fault for letting you do it. As far as I'm concerned, I have no idea what's happening.'

'Thanks Eli.'

Asher looked between the two of them; the air felt heavy with the silence, like it did before a thunderstorm.

# Lilith Descends

The knock at the door alerted Felix to her arrival. Asher looked up from his Nintendo and shot a questioning glance at his dad.

'It'll be fine,' Felix said, although he wasn't too certain. That whole morning his stomach had been plagued with swarms of butterflies, and not the nice kind you get when you fall in love. No, the feral kind that feel like they're trying to eat you from the inside out. He plastered a fake smile on his face and went to answer the door. Only upon reaching the door, did he realise that a smile was likely not the right facial expression for a man who was supposed to be suffering from a haunting.

After fixing his facial expression, he opened the door. And there she was, in all her malignant glory.

'Hello, Lilith?' he said, reaching out his hand.

'Yes, it's lovely to meet you,' she said, grasping his hand. There was an awkward moment where neither of them shook, but they both released their grip on the other after a beat.

'Thank you for coming, especially at such short notice.'

'Well, it seems that you were in dire need of help and so I was more than happy to accommodate.'

'Come on in,' he said, pushing the door wider and beckoning Lilith inside.

'Thank you.'

As Lilith walked through the doorway she cocked her head at an angle, surveying the walls and ceiling of the hall, like she was expecting a ghost to jump out at her.

'You have a lovely home,' she said.

Felix smiled at her. 'Do you want a tour, or do you want a coffee first?'

'Let's have a coffee and we can have more of a chat about what's going on here,' she said. Her scent filled the tight entrance hall to his house. Predictably, patchouli and something else woody. Her long hair was loose down her back. She wore leggings and a crop top, like she'd come straight from Pilates.

'This way,' Felix said, leading her into the kitchen.

Lilith made herself comfortable at the table and pulled out a notepad and pen from her bag. She watched Felix as he set the coffeemaker running, not attempting to make small talk. Every so often, out of the corner of his eye, Felix watched her twitch, moving her head to the side as though she'd seen something move through her peripheral vision.

Felix joined Lilith at the table, sitting at the opposite end so that they were facing each other.

'So, tell me what you want to get from my visit,' Lilith said. She picked up her pen and stared intently at him. He had the distinct feeling that he was in a job interview.

'I want everything to go back to normal,' he said. Surely that was what everybody who hired Lilith wanted.

'And what is normal to you?' she said.

'Nothing paranormal?' He hadn't intended to phrase it like a question but he was unsure about what answer she could possibly be expecting.

'Of course,' she said, writing in her notepad. Annoyingly, the writing was too small to make out from where Felix sat. 'Anything else?'

'We just want to live a normal life with nothing… spooky.'

'Well, we can certainly do that for you.' Lilith beamed beatifically at him. 'Can you tell me, again, what's been happening in your home?'

Felix launched into an explanation of the faux-paranormal activity. Cold spots, noises at night, the TV turning itself on and off, voices in the bedroom, shadowy figures, Asher's toys moving.

'And when did it start happening?' Lilith asked when she finally looked up from her notepad.

'A few months ago.'

'Can you be more specific?' She raised an eyebrow in question.

'April time, I think.' Felix chastised himself for not considering the timeframe in his plan.

'And what's your family dynamic?'

'My family dynamic?'

'Who lives here?'

'It's just me and Asher.'

Lilith jotted that down.

'What about Asher's mother?'

'She died when he was a baby,' Felix explained.

'How long ago?'

'About eleven years.' Felix swallowed the bile that had built in his throat. He hated talking about Jenna with anybody other than family. It felt impossible to do Jenna justice using only words.

'About eleven years?'

'She died on the 14th April 2012,' Felix said. He could never forget that date. He still took the day off work every year.

Felix watched as something shifted in Lilith's face.

'The anniversary of her death would have been around the same time the *paranormal activity* started?'

*Fuck*. Felix hated himself for saying 'April' when asked when the haunting had started. Any other month would have been safe but, no, he had to choose the month his wife died.

'Yes, I suppose so.'

'Have you felt her presence over the years?'

For once, Felix was able to answer truthfully. 'No. Look, I know what you're thinking, but my wife has nothing to do with this, and I'd prefer not to talk about her.'

Getting defensive wasn't going to help him. He knew that, but he couldn't stop it. He needed to put up the boundaries so that Lilith knew Jenna was off the table completely. If she even insinuated that his wife was to blame for the paranormal activity, Felix would explode.

'It's just, I tend not to believe in coincidences.'

'Are you suggesting…' Felix said through gritted teeth.

'That your wife is causing the hauntings? No, not necessarily. The loss of a loved one is a powerful thing, it can mess with our minds, make us see and hear things that aren't there. But also, I fundamentally believe that our grief is an energy and, most of the time, these instances of paranormal activity are simply down to a shift in energy in the environment. Everything has energy, and that energy has to go somewhere.'

Felix managed to nod his head.

'Your son is home?' she asked.

'Yes, he's playing on his Nintendo in the living room.'

'Mind if I have a quick chat with him?' Lilith asked.

'Yes, but don't mention his mother. Under any circumstances.'

'I respect that,' Lilith said. The sad smile on her face made Felix bristle. He didn't want her sympathy, or worse, her pity. He just wanted to expose her as the fraud she was so that all of this would be over.

# Hippy Shit Ensues

Lilith asked Asher to tell her about the paranormal activity he'd been experiencing. She didn't use the term 'paranormal activity' though. Instead, she referred to it as 'the strange things happening in your house' as though he wouldn't understand the term 'paranormal activity'. He was twelve, he wasn't stupid. The sense of relief that Felix felt when Lilith kept up her end of the bargain, by not mentioning Jenna, was almost embarrassing. The last thing he wanted was to upset Asher's life any more than he already had by bringing Lilith in to fix the imaginary ghosts.

Once Lilith had finished talking to Asher, she went back to the kitchen and began to dig through her Mary Poppins style bag. She laid various trinkets on the dining table. A bundle of what Felix assumed was sage, a stick of wood that was about as long as a pencil and about an inch in diameter, it smelled strongly of something that reminded Felix of the kind of herbs you'd get on a pizza, a palm-sized silver crucifix, a spray bottle of purple liquid, and a bottle of what looked like washing up liquid.

'Oh, one more thing,' she muttered under her breath. Once more, she dug into her bag and pulled out a cross made of sticks that looked exactly like it had come straight out of *The Blair Witch Project.*

Felix eyed her warily, wondering if she'd forgotten anything else.

'Okay, I'll make my way around the house now, focusing on the problem areas. Don't mind me if I'm quiet, I'm concentrating on feeling the vibrations of the house.'

Felix smiled and nodded, hoping that he didn't look as judgmental as he felt.

'Can you show me to the cold spot?' Lilith asked. She clutched the cross of sticks in her hand, carrying it as one might carry a weapon.

'This way,' Felix said. He led her to the top of the stairs and then moved backwards to allow her some space.

'Oh, yes, I feel that,' she said. 'Much colder.'

Felix didn't trust himself to speak and so simply dipped his chin in a small nod.

'Are there any windows open or any areas where a draft might come through?'

'No,' Felix said.

'And, just to check, your carbon monoxide detector is working, yes?'

'Yes,' Felix said.

'Good, we have to rule out all mundane explanations before we move onto the paranormal or supernatural, I'm sure you understand.'

'Of course,' Felix said. He was sure that a 'serious' paranormal investigator would check those things for themselves rather than relying on the homeowner's word, but he didn't say anything. It would be pointless seeing as the haunting was completely fabricated.

'And the room where your son's toys move?'

'His bedroom,' Felix said, opening the door at the top of the stairs.

'Cute room,' she smiled.

'Thanks,' Felix said. Not one for decorating, Felix had allowed Eli to decorate Asher's room when he grew out of the cot he'd had as a baby. It hadn't been decorated since, but Eli knew his brother well and had opted for neutral colours that wouldn't age. The only things not neutral were Asher's Pokémon bedding and the toys that lined every surface.

'Do you feel that?' Lilith said, her expression suddenly stone-faced.

'Feel what?' Felix asked.

'The energy is different in here. It shifted when we walked over the threshold. You say that your son's toys move of their own accord?'

Resisting the urge to backtrack, Felix said, 'Yes, but we never actually see them move. They're just in a different place when he looks for them.'

'And you're sure he's not moving them himself?'

'He isn't,' Felix said.

'I didn't think so. Felix, I have to be honest with you, I'm concerned about your son.'

Felix remained quiet, waiting for Lilith to continue.

'But, I will do my very best to make your house a safe place once more.'

'Thank you,' Felix said.

'Now, show me where you see the ghostly figures.'

Felix followed Lilith around the house, answering questions and trying to bite back his sarcastic comments. Once the full tour was done, Lilith went back to the dining table and began working through the tools of her trade. She began with the bundle of sage, which she called a *smudge stick*. She lit the end of it with a Bic lighter and walked around the house waving the acrid smoke in the air. Every so often, she stopped, closed her eyes, and took a long exhale. Without comment, she'd then move on. Once that was completed, she progressed to her next target. The stick. She held the lighter to the tip of it and let the end burn. Smoke curled from the orange flame.

'Palos Santos,' she said to Felix, as though that would explain what she was doing.

Lilith's eyes flickered shut. She held her breath, clenched her jaw, and blew out the flame. The end of the stick continued smoking fiercely. She took another loop of the whole house with the smoking stick. The pizza-scented smoky tendrils made Felix's stomach growl with hunger. As she took the stick on a tour of the house, she whispered *words* under her breath. 'Words' wasn't exactly the right noun for what she was doing. 'Noises' felt more appropriate.

'Om hahaha Vismaya svaha.' Over and over Lilith chorused the phrase until the words crawled under Felix's skin. When Lilith stopped in the front room and chanted, Asher shot Felix a questioning look but said nothing.

'I'm going to do some cleansing now,' Lilith said.

Felix swallowed the urge to ask what she'd been doing before.

She picked up the spray bottle and left the room, her gait full of purpose. After a second of indecision, Felix decided to stay put. Lilith returned a few minutes later and squirted the spray all over the kitchen. Puffs of water filled the air and a strong scent of lavender filled the room.

'Now I'm just going to cleanse your doorframes to prevent more evil from entering your home.'

'More evil?' Felix said before he could stop himself.

'It's a precaution. All part of the service.' Lilith smiled and picked up the bottle of what looked like washing up liquid. She dipped a hand back into her bag and grabbed a rag.

'Won't be long,' she said. Once more she exited the room.

The door to the kitchen groaned open. Asher stuck his head around it.

'How much longer will she be?' he asked.

'No idea, sorry mate,' Felix said.

Asher slid back into the living room without another word.

Not for the first time, Felix wondered what kind of a father he was to bring some strange weirdo into their home.

Felix stared at his hands and waited for Lilith to return, pondering his parenting skills.

'Just these doors to do,' Lilith said entering the room.

She bent down and wiped a cloth over the door leading into the living room. She did the same to the door that led to the back garden.

'All done. What I tend to suggest is that we wait and see if the cleansing has done its job. Hopefully, that's all it takes. If it doesn't work, give me a call and I'll come back, and then we'll try something more extreme.'

'Thank you,' Felix said. 'I appreciate your help.'

'Thanks for trusting me. I'll just pack up my bits and pieces and I'll be out of your hair.'

With all of her bits and pieces back in her bag, Lilith smiled at Felix.

'It was lovely to meet you. I will send the invoice when I get home. I ask for payment to be sent within 24 hours.'

Felix nodded his head. 'I'll pay straight away.'

'Great, thanks.'

Felix walked Lilith to the front door.

'Bye,' she said, as she headed off down the garden path to her brand-new Range Rover.

# A Stereotypical Haunting: Part Two

The rest of the day passed in a lazy haze. They lounged around, the TV creating background noise as Asher played on his Nintendo and Felix opened his first book of the summer holidays. Teaching didn't leave as much room for reading for pleasure as he would have liked and, throughout the school year, he found himself reading the assigned texts over and over again instead. He needed to know them inside out in order to teach them effectively. And, after spending his whole days surrounded by books and their 'messages', he usually couldn't find it in him to pick up another book when he got home. An occupational hazard, he supposed. His genre of choice was horror. Anything bordering on *literary fiction* (he hated that phrase) meant that he'd be searching for hidden meanings and literary devices. Horror allowed his brain to switch off fully.

As much as he tried, Felix couldn't retain the words he was reading. His mind was absorbed by Lilith. He'd done what he intended to do, and spent an eye-watering amount of money in doing so, but what happened next? How would he tell the public that she was a fraud and that she'd provided a fake service, readily believing (and encouraging) his lies? If Felix had genuinely believed that he was being haunted, then the ways in which she'd reacted and the services she had provided would only have served to deepen his delusions. If a person believes that they're being haunted, the only logical explanation is that they're mentally ill… or that their house is creaky or leaky. Lilith, without any qualms, would have fed his delusions, validating them and making them feel like a reality. It was the behaviour of a person with no morals, but how could he prove that? He really should have thought more about how to prove Lilith was a fake before inviting her into his home, maybe set up cameras or something, but it was too late for that and he had no intentions of paying another grand to bring her back.

Putting his book to the side, Felix unlocked his phone and typed into Google; 'reporting a business scam.' There were options aplenty. Contact the police, Citizens Advice, or Trading Standards. Other options included a couple of charities that specialised in scams and fraud, or some solicitor's firms. You could even report a business through the GOV.UK website. The first point of call would be filling in the online form to report Lilith to Trading Standards, and then through the GOV.UK website. He was a 'customer' and therefore had a legitimate interest in reporting the business. As a customer, one who'd paid a hell of a lot of money at that, the organisations should take his reports seriously. Hopefully, the outcome would be that Lilith wouldn't take advantage of any more grieving or mentally ill people. He could go to sleep feeling relatively good about his life choices. After filling in the forms, which only took about fifteen minutes (Felix chose not to read too much into that) he noticed Asher yawning.

'Time for bed,' Felix said. 'Go brush your teeth and get your jammies on.'

Without protesting, Asher saved his game and turned it off. He was always such a good kid. Felix had no idea what he'd done to deserve that. Many kids Asher's age were tyrants, but Asher did as he was told. Maybe he was a little too into his games, but the world was changing. Maybe he'd go into game designing or something. Who was Felix to stand in his way?

Felix did a quick tidy of the downstairs and then went to check on Asher. Tidying downstairs before bed was something Jenna had instilled in him. *'You can't go to bed with a messy house,'* she'd always said. It used to drive him crazy. Now, he'd give anything for her to tell him to tidy up. Since her death, he'd never once gone to bed with a messy house. Not even in the days and weeks directly after her death.

Asher was propped up in bed, a book open on his lap. Warmth flooded over Felix as he looked at his son.

'Can we read a chapter before bed?' he asked.

Another tradition that remained from Jenna. Bedtime had been her domain and she always read a book to Asher before he went to sleep. Even from being a brand-new baby. Felix had laughed and told her that reading a book to a two-day-old baby was pointless. Jenna retorted that it was never too early to foster a love of books, and Felix had found himself unable to argue with her. Since then, most nights, Asher had been read to before bed. It was a tradition that he hoped Asher would never grow out of, but Felix knew that this tradition had to come to an end soon. He would allow that to happen on Asher's terms.

Asher pushed himself up against the wall so that Felix could squish onto the single bed beside him. They were currently halfway through a Goosebumps book, one about a ventriloquist dummy that comes to life and causes mayhem. Although Asher was reading well above where he should be for his age, he laid back and allowed his dad to read to him, the words washing over him and lulling him to sleep as they always did.

'Asher,' a voice whispered in his ear.

Asher awoke alone in bed. The covers were warm and musty.

'Dad?' he said into the blackness of his room. He blinked, trying to see through the dimness. He couldn't see his dad anywhere. 'Dad?' he asked again.

Turning on the lamp on his bedside table, Asher waited for his eyes to adjust. After deciding he must have dreamt his dad's voice, he turned off the lamp and tried to get back to sleep. As he was slipping off, he heard his dad call for him.

'Asher.'

The voice was more urgent this time.

Asher turned the lamp back on, feeling the unfamiliar prickle of annoyance at his dad.

'What?' Asher said, projecting his voice so that it would carry out of the room.

'Asher,' his dad repeated.

'What the hell?' Asher muttered under his breath. He threw back the covers and swung his feet over the end of the bed. The floor was cold under his feet. Dad said that the hardwood floor was *original* so they couldn't get rid of it. Uncle Eli had carpets in his bedroom there and Asher much preferred that. The floor sighed with each step he took. Pushing open his bedroom door, he peered into the hallway.

'Dad?' he said again.

He was greeted with silence.

Just as Asher was about to turn around and head back to bed, feeling irritated but sleepy, his dad shouted again. The voice came from downstairs, but all the lights were off downstairs.

'Dad?' Asher whisper-shouted down the stairs. He tiptoed closer to the top step. A shiver slid through his body. It was freezing.

He turned back to look at his dad's bedroom door. It was closed, as it always was when his dad was sleeping. But Asher was sure that the voice had come from downstairs. He reached tentatively for the light switch that worked the bulb at the bottom of the staircase. Before his finger made contact, he saw a shadow move through the dark at the bottom of the stairs. It was tall, about the same size as his dad, but its body wasn't the right shape, and it was almost see-through.

'Asher?' The word came from behind him. Asher whirled around, losing his footing. His dad reached out and caught his arm, pulling him to safety.

Asher's heart tried to beat out of his chest. It was a close call. If his dad hadn't been there to pull him back… He turned around and looked down the stairs. Nothing there. Well, nothing that he could see at least.

'What's wrong? What are you doing up?' His dad's voice was painted with concern. When he was worried, his voice changed completely and it sounded like he was talking to a little kid, not an almost-teenager.

'You shouted me,' Asher said. 'But you were downstairs.'

'I was in my bedroom, asleep. I didn't…' He paused and Asher watched as a visible shudder shook his body. 'It's bloody freezing.'

'It's the top step,' Asher said.

To test the theory, Asher stepped to the top of the stairs again. And then moved a few steps back. He repeated the action a couple of times before he was satisfied that this theory was correct.

'That doesn't make sense. Where's the draft coming from? Did you open the bathroom window?'

'No, I didn't. Dad, we told Lilith that the top step was a cold spot.'

'Funny coincidence,' his dad said, although his face didn't look as sure as his voice sounded.

'I saw something at the bottom of the stairs,' Asher said.

'What?' His dad tilted his head to the side the same way Specs did when he was trying to understand what you were asking him to do.

'It was a shadow. It moved across the bottom of the stairs like it was floating.'

'You must still have been dreaming. I should never have invited Lilith here. It's upset you. I'm sorry, Ash. I really am.'

'I wasn't asleep.'

'Sometimes we see things that aren't really there in the dark. It's our mind playing tricks on us.'

'I know what I saw.' Asher's voice sounded like steel. He *knew* what he'd seen. Hell, his dad saw dead people all the time, but when Asher saw a ghost, or whatever it was, *that* was impossible.

'Let's get you back to bed,' his dad said. The conversation was over.

Asher allowed his dad to lead him back into the bedroom. He didn't know whether to tell his dad that the duvet had been moved from where he'd left it on the bed. It was now all the way over at the other side of the room.

# All In Your Head

Felix felt like ice-cold water had flooded his veins. He laid in bed and attempted to coerce his body to sleep, and failed miserably. What Asher had said… the cold spot, the figures at the bottom of the stairs, it was too much. He'd fucked up massively. The lies he'd told Lilith seemed to have pervaded Asher's mind, seeping into his subconscious and forcing him to see things that weren't there. If Jenna were here, she'd be livid. He lay there with his eyes open, staring at the ceiling. It was barely quarter past two, but Felix was certain sleep would continue to evade him for the rest of the night. He released a ragged sigh and sat up.

A shadow stood tall in the corner of his bedroom. Rubbing his eyes to clear any residual sleep, Felix studied the shape. Not quite a man. Unable to rip his eyes away from the shadowed form, Felix continued to glare at it, trying to decipher which of his belongings could morph into something so sinister. It wasn't hanging clothes or his dressing gown. It wasn't *anything*. The ice-cold water that had flooded his veins turned solid. He hadn't experienced fear like this since he was a child and had woken up from an unintelligible nightmare.

Felix fumbled for the switch on his bedside lamp. A relic from Jenna. Tiffany style with a tiny switch on its neck. With his pulse throbbing in his temples, Felix kept his eyes on the shape in the corner. Irrationally, he thought that if he looked away, it would pounce.

'Fuck,' he mumbled, unable to find the damned switch. In his desperation, he knocked the lamp off the bedside table and onto the floor. 'Shit!' he snarled.

The shadow remained still, daring him to look away. If he'd been a child, Felix would have closed his eyes tightly and told himself that this was just a dream. As an adult, he knew that trick wouldn't work.

The shushing sound of a whispered voice emanated from the corner of the room, from the *thing* that stood in the shadow. He had to stand up. He had to turn the light on. But he couldn't. He just couldn't.

The whispering grew louder and louder until it flooded his senses. Felix couldn't make out the words it was saying. It wasn't English as far as he could tell. The voice filled the space, eating up all of the air in the room. Suffocating him. His thoughts swam and his vision zoomed in and out. Struggling to his feet, Felix fell forwards onto his hands and knees, hitting the floor with a thud. He tried to push himself to his feet but dizziness overcame him.

*What the fuck is happening?* He wasn't sure whether he said the words aloud or whether they remained trapped in his mind.

Crawling to his closed bedroom door took every ounce of energy he had left. Each movement caused his vision to condense and his mind to fog.

*Get to the door.*

Unable to turn his head to see the figure in the corner, Felix powered onwards. The whispering was incessant, drilling into his skull. A wave of relief washed over him as his fingers found the doorknob. The metal was cold against his skin. From all fours, he turned the knob and pulled the door open. He rolled to the side to allow the landing light to flood into the room. The blurriness in his brain cleared. The whispering stopped. The shadow no longer stood in the corner. Embarrassment replaced the feeling of relief. Using the doorframe, Felix pulled himself up. Standing in his doorway, he saw Asher looking up at him. He hadn't heard his son approach.

'Hey,' Felix said, his voice rough. He cleared his throat and tried again. 'Couldn't sleep?'

'I heard you shouting,' Asher said. His voice was calm and matter-of-fact.

'Bad dream.' Felix grimaced. If Jenna was buried, she'd be rolling in her grave at the thought of how much he was fucking up right now.

'Oh,' Asher said. 'Dad?'

'Yes,' Felix replied. His heart hammered in his chest. He tried to slow his breathing and compose himself.

'Can I sleep in your bed?' Asher said. He looked so young.

'Of course,' Felix said.

In a voice so low Felix could barely hear it, Asher said, 'When I woke up, all of my toys had moved.'

# Hackles Rising

When his phone rang, Eli expected it to be work related. Nobody ever rang him unless it was a client. Despite being in his thirties, he still hated talking on the phone with a passion. He did it when he had to, but otherwise avoided it. When he saw the caller ID, he calmed. Felix.

'You busy today?' Felix asked.

'I can move some things around,' Eli responded. One of the joys of being self-employed was that he could always move his graphic design projects around. He left himself enough time with his deadlines that he could have the occasional spur-of-the-moment morning off.

'Can you come here?' Felix said. There was something about his voice that sounded like nails on a chalkboard. It unsettled him.

'Sure. Everything okay?' he said.

'Yeah. Actually, no, not really. Something fucked up is happening.'

Under different circumstances, Eli would have laughed at his brother's language.

'I'll be there in an hour.' Eli hung up the phone and turned to look at Specs, whose expectant tail was thumping against the carpet.

'Looks like we're going to see Asher,' he said to the dog.

The word 'Asher' triggered Specs who leapt up from his spot and placed his paws on Eli's stomach. The gesture said, 'Really?!'

'Dumb dog,' Eli said affectionately, scratching Specs's oversized staffy head.

Eli walked to his brother's house. It was only ten minutes away, plus it had the added bonus of constituting a walk for his lazy dog. Specs wasn't one for walks but the second they turned the corner onto Felix's street, he knew that his owner had been telling the truth when he'd said 'Asher' earlier, and he picked up the pace.

'Slow down, Specs,' Eli said as Specs pulled him along the pavement and up to Felix's front door. Eli slipped his key into the lock and opened the door.

'Hello,' he called into the house, unhooking Specs's lead and letting him free. He barrelled up the stairs and a few seconds later he heard Asher giggling.

Eli walked into the kitchen to find Felix hunched over the dining table. Purple bags hung under his eyes. He stared into the depths of the coffee in front of him.

'Rough night?' Eli said. He walked over to the coffee machine and poured himself a cup before joining his brother at the table.

'Felix?' Eli prompted.

'Shit, sorry,' Felix said, looking up and meeting Eli's eyes.

'You look like you've seen a ghost,' he said. An inside joke that usually gleaned laughter from his brother. He was always seeing ghosts.

Instead of laughing, Felix shook his head and rolled his eyes. 'You don't know the half of it.'

'What? Eli pushed.

'Last night was… I don't know how to explain it.' Felix's skin had taken on a green tinge.

'What happened?'

'It was so weird,' Felix said.

Becoming impatient, Eli reached a hand across the table and tapped his brother's. 'Just spit it out,' he said.

'I woke up and found Asher at the top of the stairs. He said that he'd seen a figure moving at the bottom. I grabbed him just as he was about to fall.'

'Woah,' Eli exhaled. That wasn't what he'd anticipated.

'There was a cold spot at the top of the stairs too,' Felix continued.

Eli wanted to say, *That could have been a draft. Did you leave a window open?* But his brother was so freaked out, he didn't dare.

'I couldn't get back to sleep after. Not properly anyway. I heard whispers. Well, they weren't whispers exactly. They were loud. Like, loud-loud. They echoed off the walls of my room and I couldn't think straight. It was like this fog clouded my brain.' Felix shook his head more vigorously. 'I saw a figure too. In the corner of my room.'

Felix placed his head in his hands, his elbows propped on the table.

'Felix…' Eli said. He couldn't think of anything else to say.

'I'm not crazy,' Felix said.

'I know that,' Eli said.

'I broke the lamp trying to get out of bed and I had to crawl to my door because my legs wouldn't fucking work.' Each word sounded strained as though Felix had to force it from his mouth. 'When I opened the door, everything went back to normal.'

'It was probably a night-'

'Don't you dare say it was a nightmare,' Felix said, his voice as hard as stone.

'But-' Eli said.

Felix didn't need to say another word to stop Eli in his tracks.

'If it's not a nightmare, then what was it?' Eli said eventually after staring down Felix.

'I don't know. But it was real. Fucking terrifying,' Felix said, biting his lip.

'It started after you called Lilith,' Eli said, aware that his words weren't particularly helpful. He'd told Felix not to call her. It would only ever end badly.

'And it was exactly what I described to her. What happened was word-for-word what we told her had happened. At least at first. The stuff in my bedroom was different.'

Eli blinked, not sure what to say.

'What should I do?' Felix said.

'I have no idea. I mean, you could call Mum, but she'd kill you herself. You don't mess with paranormal stuff, she's always said that. All you'd get is, *you should have known better.* And, while I agree with her, it's not helpful right now. The only other option is to call Lilith and find out if she's fucking with you.'

'How could she possibly be fucking with me?' Felix asked.

'Well, you said that last night happened exactly as you told her, and she charges per day, right? Did you leave her alone? Could she have rigged something to happen?'

'No. I mean, I don't think so,' Felix said. 'How could she have made me see things? Hear things?'

'She's a charlatan, maybe she drugged you.'

'Be reasonable,' Felix said, his bloodshot eyes staring into Eli's.

'You seeing the dead is reasonable? A haunting is reasonable? But a con artist drugging somebody to make more money isn't?'

Felix surveyed his brother. He had a valid point.

'Maybe try to get some sleep? I'll watch Ash while you have a nap, you look rough as fuck. You might be able to think more clearly after.'

'Thanks,' Felix said, sarcasm oozing from his voice.

'Yesterday could well have triggered some things, that's all I'm saying. Just try to chill out and relax and we can talk more about it later.'

'Maybe you're right,' Felix said, and Eli almost fell off his chair.

'I am right. I'm always right. Get on the sofa and I'll wake you up in a couple of hours.'

'Thank you, Eli,' Felix said. The sincerity in Felix's words knocked the breath out of Eli. His brother was well and truly scared.

A single loud bark, like a snap of thunder, shocked them both to attention. Specs didn't bark like that. Not ever.

Another bark, followed by a low rumbling growl.

Eli led the way, sprinting up the staircase and into Asher's bedroom.

'What's-' Eli started, looking around the room.

Asher stood in the middle of his bedroom, hands up in an 'I'm innocent' gesture. Specs's snarl was aimed at the corner of the room. Nothing was there but Asher's washing basket.

'Specs,' Eli said, making his way over to the dog. Specs paid no attention to his owner, and instead, arched his back, the raised hackles on his back growing in prominence. Eli had never once seen Specs behave like this.

'Specs, buddy, what's wrong?' Eli said, approaching Specs slowly so as not to startle him. He turned to Asher. 'What happened before Specs started-'

'I don't know,' Asher interrupted. 'He just started barking and snarling at nothing.'

Eli nodded, not sure what could have upset Specs so badly.

'Hey Specs,' Asher said, edging closer to the dog.

Specs turned around and fixed his eyes on the boy. 'Come here,' Asher said.

Asher's words broke the spell. Specs whined by way of an apology and approached him, nuzzling at Asher's legs with his head, much like a cat would.

'What the hell was that about?' Felix said to Eli.

'I have no idea,' Eli said. 'Something scared the shit out of him.'

'You said a bad word,' Asher said, raising his eyebrow at his uncle and smiling mischievously.

'My bad,' Eli said. His nerves were on fire.

# Whispers in the Night

Felix didn't manage to nap that afternoon. Adrenaline coursed through his body, preventing him from remaining still long enough to fall asleep. Whatever had scared Specs was in his house. He was a rational guy, other than seeing spirits of the dead, but the last twenty-four hours had pushed him to his limits. He felt like he was careening down the side of a mountain, an avalanche nipping at his heels. Eli stayed until after dinner, and then had reluctantly gone home, after offering for Felix and Asher to stay the night at his house. Eli already thought Felix was crazy, taking him up on the offer would only serve to confirm that. Felix had no intention of proving his brother right.

In the harsh light of day, Felix *did* wonder if maybe last night had been a figment of their imaginations thanks to the stress caused by inviting Lilith into their home. Maybe it was some strange psychological response to the trauma of losing Jenna, and never having seen her presence, that had triggered the hallucinations. As for Asher, he was a little boy with an over-active imagination. You saw it all the time. It was Felix's fault that Asher had the nightmare, Felix had put the ideas in his head. And Felix almost managed to convince himself that this was true. Almost.

Asher went to bed at his usual time of 8.30 pm. He went through his nighttime ritual alone, like he did most evenings: shower, pyjamas on, brush teeth, and get into bed.

'Can we have another chapter, Dad?' he asked, holding up the Goosebumps book.

'What about if we read something different?' Felix suggested. Goosebumps, after their *episode* last night, didn't feel like the best choice.

'It's only a book,' Asher said, smiling. 'You always said I could read *anything* I wanted to.'

Asher was right. Felix was a vehement supporter of allowing children and young people to read whatever they wanted to, putting limitations on their reading habits would only stifle their love of reading, and as an English lecturer, that made his job a thousand times harder.

'Sure,' Felix said, in awe of his son's resilience.

'It's only a book, dad,' Asher repeated, grinning from ear to ear. 'Don't let it scare you.'

'Thank you,' Felix said, placing a hand on Asher's wet hair and allowing it to trail down. 'I appreciate the support.'

Asher snorted. 'Come on then,' he said. 'Get to it.'

'Your wish is my command,' Felix said and launched into the next chapter of the story.

With each sentence, Asher snuggled in closer to Felix. With each word, Felix's eyes grew heavier, lulled to sleep by the scent of his son and the sound of his own voice.

He awoke later to the noise of Asher's gentle snores. A steady rhythm that felt as familiar as his own heartbeat. The bed was warm, but not uncomfortably so. His head rested close to Asher's, their temples touching.

'Kitty?' Asher said.

Felix turned to look at his son. He must have spoken in his sleep because his eyelids were fluttering as though he was dreaming.

'Kitty.' Asher's mouth didn't move. Felix lay as still as a corpse, trying to understand what was happening. His sleep-addled brain couldn't put the pieces together in a way that made sense. It was Asher's voice speaking to him. He was sure of it, and yet Asher slept like the dead next to him.

'Kitty.' It was no longer Asher's voice. He'd recognise this voice anywhere.

'Jenna?' Felix sat up and turned to look around the room. Hearing the pet name she'd called him since their first date felt like a dagger in his side. She'd joked that Felix was a cat's name, and the nickname had stuck. She never called him anything else.

'Kitty, I've missed you.' Felix's eyes whirled around the room trying to find Jenna.

'Where are you?' Felix said, the lump in his throat made it hard to speak.

'I'm right here,' the voice said to his right.

He turned his head but couldn't see her.

'I can't see you,' he said, desperation leaked into his words.

'I'm here, Kitty,' she said. This time, the voice came from behind him. He turned and saw nothing but the wall Asher's bed was pressed up against.

*Kitty.*

*Kitty.*

*Kitty.*

*Kitty.*

Jenna's voice echoed from all the corners of the room. Each time, Felix searched for her. His head swivelled in the direction of each word, desperate to see Jenna.

*Kitty.*

*Kitty.*

*Kitty.*

The words grew louder and quicker. Cacophonous. Bouncing around the room like a squash ball. Felix couldn't find her. He looked and looked, following the words with his eyes. She wasn't there. But she *had* to be. She was speaking to him.

'Kitty,' the word was slow, steady, the same cadence with which Jenna had spoken.

'You invited it in,' she said.

# Remembering Mummy

The photographs were scattered all over the living room floor. This was one of Jenna's foibles that had paid off. She was an avid believer that photographs were supposed to be printed off and held, not kept on phones and hard drives. The photographs spanned Jenna's whole life, from being a baby. The ones of Felix began to appear sporadically toward the end of Jenna's high school years, when they'd started dating. Felix hadn't kept the habit up and so the series of photographs finished with the documentation of the first year of Asher's life. There were, of course, still photos of Jenna on the walls and various sideboards too; their wedding photo and photos of them as a family, but the majority of Jenna's life was documented in the box that lived under Felix's bed.

When Asher had asked to look through the photos, Felix hesitated for the first time ever. Usually, he jumped at the chance to look through the photos with Asher, telling him stories about his mother, but after what had happened last night, and the night before for that matter, he wasn't entirely convinced that a trip down memory lane was a good idea. As he'd started to stutter, Asher had said, 'Please,' and that was all it took. Moments later, the photos were splayed over the living room floor.

'Tell me about what Uncle Eli did,' Asher demanded. In his hand, he held a photo of Eli and Felix together at Felix and Jenna's wedding. The story he was referring to happened during the evening portion of the wedding, and it always sent Asher into fits of giggles. Eli was supposed to give a speech but became otherwise preoccupied with Jenna's best friend, Martin, and missed his cue. Felix's mother had found them together in the disabled toilet. The version of the story that Felix told Asher was the PG version with the word 'kissing' substituted for what had actually happened. Still, Asher loved the story, and poking fun at Eli, and so Felix told the story for what felt like the hundredth time. It finished with Asher laughing at the prospect of Uncle Eli doing something as untoward as kissing a boy in the toilets. Eli had never hidden his sexuality which meant, to Asher, the fact that Uncle Eli had boyfriends, not girlfriends, was as normal as anything else in life, as well it should be in Felix's mind. As long as Eli was happy, Felix was happy. The story was still told at most family gatherings, after a couple of drinks, and Eli was always a good sport about it.

Together, Asher and Felix laid the photographs out in a rough order, starting with Jenna as a baby and ending with one of her and

Asher a couple of weeks before she died. Asher knew the story behind each photo, but still asked Felix to re-tell them.

'Why did Mummy have a pot on her arm?'

'Who is that with Mummy?'

'Why did you have that haircut?' *That* question stung particularly, seeing as Felix was now balding and would have killed to have the One Direction/Zac Efron haircut back. As they reminisced, the hard rock of anxiety that sat in Felix's chest began to ebb away.

A beam of sunlight broke through the living room window, highlighting the smooth skin of Asher's face. It bounced from the tips of his dark hair, casting it in a thousand shades of brown.

'Can we watch the video?' Asher asked when they'd finally worked their way through the whole box of photos.

'Sure,' Felix said. As he stood, his knees popped and ground. He pulled his wedding DVD out of the plastic envelope and put it into the Xbox. After a few seconds, he grabbed the controller and pressed 'play'.

The video began with Jenna getting ready along with her bridesmaids and her mum. The last time Felix had seen Jenna's mum was the funeral. She'd emailed him a few days after saying that it was *too hard* to see Asher after her daughter's death; the same went for Jenna's father. Felix left them to it. He'd wanted to scream and protest – *how do you think I feel, she's my wife?* – but he didn't. He said that the door was always open if they changed their mind. They hadn't. When Asher had first asked why he didn't see Grandma and

Grandad Stokes anymore, after watching the wedding video one Sunday morning, Felix told him a diluted version of the truth. That they were still very sad that Jenna had died and they found it difficult to be around people, or things, that reminded them of her. When Asher had replied with 'But you're sad too,' Felix felt his heart break all over again. Asher no longer asked about them.

Father and son stared at Jenna as she laughed with her bridesmaids, drank asti, and cried when her father came into the room. There were no shots of Felix and Eli getting ready, all the attention had been (rightfully) on Jenna. The scene changed and focused on Felix and Eli, who both stood in silent panic at the front of the pavilion. The music started and the camera turned to face Jenna once again, veil over her gorgeous face and arm-in-arm with her dad. They walked down the aisle slowly, the biggest grin plastered to her face. Jenna didn't cry, not once. Instead, she beamed. Felix was the one who cried, much to the pleasure of their selected friends and family. The vows were said. The aisle was walked once more. The camera zoomed in on the happy couple's faces. Both Felix and Asher knew the video by heart. When the first glitch occurred, they looked to one another to check if the other had seen it too.

'The DVD is probably getting old,' Felix said, not removing his eyes from Jenna.

'Sure,' Asher said.

The camera continued to follow Felix and Jenna up the aisle. The glitch happened again. Jenna's face contorted, her mouth stretched downwards in a mimic of a Halloween horror mask. Her eyes no longer smiled, they widened in horror.

'What-' Asher began to speak.

'I don't know,' Felix interrupted.

Jenna's face returned to normal. Felix crawled closer to the TV. His blood turned to ice despite the hot summer breeze leaking in through the window. He was so close that he could reach out and touch the screen, touch Jenna, but he didn't. He couldn't. The video continued like nothing happened. The pair of them walked out of the church toward the waiting throng of confetti-bearing guests.

Jenna's face morphed again. The mouth elongated in a silent scream. Her eyes flew wide. The picture froze on that. The camera zoomed into Jenna. *This* wasn't how the video went. They didn't stop. They walked through the confetti and kissed when they reached the end of the garden path. Static began to build in the black recesses of Jenna's gaping mouth. Felix felt his body move closer to the TV. Jenna's eyes blinked rapidly. Something began to crawl out from her darkened mouth. Jenna's neck shuddered as though she was coughing, choking, but she made no noise. Her neck pulsated, gipping. Tears leaked from her eyes. From deep within her neck, the liquid began to arise. Pitch black. Thick and oozing. It dribbled down Jenna's chin, neck, and onto the lacy folds of her dress. The liquid spurted and stuttered, turning the white dress a murky and mottled shade of brown.

*Blood.* It had to be blood.

Jenna's face snapped back to normal. Shiny, happy, bright smiles stared out at Felix.

'Dad,' Asher's voice almost broke through his consciousness. 'Daddy!' he said louder.

Until Asher spoke, Felix had forgotten that he was there.

His son was sobbing, silent tears dripping down his face and onto the floor.

'What happened to Mummy?' he said.

'I don't know,' Felix admitted. 'That wasn't real. That didn't happen. It wasn't like that. We were both happy. It was the best day.'

'Then why did she do that?'

'I don't know. I don't know.' Felix repeated the words over and over again, pulling his son against him and methodically stroking his hair.

*What the fuck is happening?* he thought.

# Multi-Sensory Experience

Asher felt like he'd never fall asleep. Every time he closed his eyes, he saw his mummy's face stretch and gape, and then something black came out of her mouth. He'd pretended that he hadn't been scared because he didn't want to upset his dad. Asher knew that the video had upset his dad too, and he didn't want to make the situation worse, so, after they turned the TV off, Asher decided to never mention it again. Dad hadn't tried to talk about it either. It was like they'd agreed, without words, that the video never happened.

Dad had already read a chapter of Goosebumps to Asher, and had gone back downstairs. He could hear the muffled sound of voices on the TV. It was comforting to know that Dad was awake. That way, if anything happened, Asher was safe. Dad would take care of him.

Asher pulled the covers up to his chin. His breath warmed the thin summer duvet.

As much as he wanted to pretend that everything was okay. Asher *knew* that something messed up was happening in the house. He'd read enough Goosebumps books, and watched enough scary movies, to know that ghosts were real. Plus, Dad saw spirits too, so there was no denying that those kinds of things existed.

Closing his eyes tightly, Asher willed sleep to come.

*Fall asleep now. Fall asleep now.* He said to himself over and over again.

It didn't work. He'd never had any trouble falling asleep. Not before Lilith came to their house. Lilith had changed everything. The house didn't feel the same as it had before she visited. It felt wrong.

Asher told himself not to think about her. He rolled onto his right side, staring at the wall, and attempted to get comfy.

'Asher, baby?' It was a woman's voice. A voice he only recognised from a wedding video played over and over again.

'Mummy?' Asher breathed.

'Asher, baby, it's me. I've missed you so much.'

Asher rolled over quickly, sitting up in his bed. The covers bunched around his legs.

'Where are you?' Asher said. He looked all around his room but couldn't see her anywhere. Excitement and trepidation flooded through him. If Dad could see spirits, then why couldn't he? It would be amazing to see his mum in real life. He loved her so much it hurt, even if he didn't remember her.

'I'm here, sweetie, can't you see me?' It sounded like the voice came from the foot of the bed.

'I'll turn on my lamp,' Asher said, reaching out to press the switch.

When the light flickered on, Asher still couldn't see anybody but the bottom of his bed was depressed, like somebody was sitting on it.

'I still can't see you,' Asher moaned.

'But you know I'm here, right?' his mum said.

'Yes,' Asher said. He could feel his mother there. Not physically, he couldn't reach out and touch her, but he knew that she was there. Maybe that was his secret power. Dad could see spirits, but Asher could only hear them.

'I'm so proud of you,' she said. 'You're so smart, and kind, and handsome. Just like your daddy.'

'Where have you been? Dad said you haven't visited him.' He desperately wanted to see her, to feel her touch.

'You've both done so well that I didn't want to upset you, but now you're struggling. You both need me to help you.'

'You can help us?' Asher balled his fists into the duvet cover.

'I can, my sweet boy. Something isn't right in this house, you know that, don't you? She brought it in. That woman brought it in.'

'Brought what in?'

'Something evil.'

'But you'll keep us safe?'

'I will, baby. I will. Just go to sleep and let me keep you safe. Lay down and close your eyes.'

The lamp turned off without Asher touching it. He smiled thinking of his mum turning it off for him, the way Dad did before he went to sleep.

'Shhh,' his mum said.

Asher jumped as he felt a hand against his hair.

The shushing continued, and his mother's hand stroked his messy hair. 'Such a beautiful boy,' she said.

Asher fell asleep in minutes with a contented smile on his face.

Felix fell asleep before his head hit the pillow. He was emotionally exhausted; physically drained. He needed sleep, and sleep welcomed him with open arms. The dream started slowly, the way most dreams did. Felix couldn't remember where the dream began, but only how it ended. He was driving along a lonely road; streetlights illuminated the ground sporadically, not enough to light the way. The car's headlights barely broke through the murk. Felix squinted but could barely see the road in front of him. He didn't see the oncoming car before it was too late. The two cars collided head-on. Felix was thrown out of his seat, the seatbelt failing to hold him from slamming against the steering wheel. His temple hit the window. A flash of light blinded him. The smell of blood, rain, and grass combined into a heady mixture. He tried to move but couldn't. He was stuck. Maybe he was also upside down, or sideways, he couldn't tell. Moving his hand, he attempted to find the seatbelt release. Each millimetre he moved sent white-hot pain down his arm and across his chest. The stench of blood was thick in the air. He began to feel heavy. His eyes fluttered closed. Nothing made sense. He couldn't grasp reality. Had he been in an accident? Was he dying? His body burned as though it had been doused with acid. He smelled acrid smoke but couldn't see any flames. He forced his eyes open again only for them to fall shut. He was so tired. He needed to sleep, he needed the pain to stop. He needed to…

Felix shot upright in bed. Cold sweat drenched his body from head to toe. His breathing came in gulps as he tried to steady himself. The nightmare had been so real. He reached for the bedside lamp before remembering that he'd broken it yesterday. The memory was grounding, bringing him back to reality. But the dream had been a reality when it had happened to Jenna. It happened exactly like the doctor had told him. The head-on collision, the car flipping, Jenna bleeding out, the car setting alight and burning her body to a crisp before she could be released from it. Nobody should die alone, especially not Jenna, who had been so selfless and kind.

Felix had never dreamed about Jenna's death before. He dreamed about *her* although those dreams had petered out over the years, but he'd never dreamed of the way she'd died. Tears bubbled in his eyes. He tried so hard not to think of her dying alone and scared and confused and in pain. He allowed himself to cry silently, shoulders shaking. The pain overwhelmed him so completely that he wasn't sure he'd ever feel normal again. He knew that grief worked in strange ways. It wasn't linear, and you never got over it.

Until he'd brought Lilith into his life, he'd thought that he was okay. He had more good days than bad and rarely found himself sobbing over Jenna anymore. But that dream, that dream was so real.

*Stress.* He decided. It had been brought on by the stress of the last crazy couple of days. Once the tears dried up, he wiped his face with the palms of his hands and stood up. Asher. When life got too much, Asher brought him back to earth. He just wanted to peep in and see his son, and then he'd be able to relax. Maybe he'd get a snack and a glass of milk before he went back to bed, that usually set him back on an even keel.

Without turning on the bedroom light, Felix crept out of his room, not wanting to wake Asher. He opened Asher's bedroom door slightly and stuck his head in. The smell hit him with force, knocking him back. Jenna's perfume. The perfume he'd bought her for every birthday, every Christmas, every anniversary. She wouldn't wear anything else. *Chloe.* He could picture the ribbed glass bottle with the ribbon around the neck.

Asher slept soundly, his chest rising and falling. But the smell made Felix feel sick to his stomach. He gagged. It was so strong, the way Jenna used to spray it before they went out on a date night or a special occasion. Felix used to joke that it was wasteful and she'd stick her tongue out at him and squirt the perfume on her wrist or neck one more time.

The logical part of his brain thought that maybe Asher had found an old bottle lying around somewhere. But Felix knew the logical part of his brain was wrong this time. Something in this

house was intent on making him feel like he was going crazy. He closed the door and sank down to the floor behind it. The smell of the perfume lingered in the air. Maybe he *was* going crazy.

# Mummy Hurt Me

Coffee. Without it, Felix wouldn't have been able to function. By the time Asher walked downstairs, Felix was already on his third cup. Asher wore short blue pyjamas with a repeating pattern of white staffies; a present from Eli for his birthday. The dogs looked just like Specs and so Asher loved the PJs. The bruises down Asher's arms looked like finger marks, the kind that kids got if you grabbed them too hard. They hadn't been there when Asher went to bed.

'What have you done to your arms?' Felix said, walking over to Asher and kneeling in front of him to inspect the bruises.

'I thought it was a dream,' Asher said, 'but it wasn't.'

'What do you mean?' Felix said. The bruises on Asher's body ran down his legs too. Felix lifted up Asher's shirt, bruises marked his torso.

'Mummy hurt me.'

'What are you talking about?' Felix said, certain he'd misheard.

'Mummy did it.'

'Mummy can't hurt you, Ash. You know that.'

Tears began to stream down Asher's face. 'But she did.'

'Sit down and tell me what happened.' Felix guided Asher to a dining chair and knelt in front of him. He searched Asher's eyes for an explanation, but found nothing.

'What happened?'

'I thought I was asleep,' Asher said. 'But I wasn't. I was dreaming about Mummy. She was stroking my hair and whispering to me. It was nice. I could smell her, she smelled pretty, but I couldn't see her. Not at first.' Asher took a huge gulp of air, tears still falling down his blotchy face.

He continued, 'And then she was there. She looked just like she did in the video, at the end when her face went funny. Her mouth was so big and her eyes looked scared. And then she pinched my leg, hard. I asked her to stop, but she wouldn't.' Asher's body began to shake with sobs. 'She kept nipping me all over my body and saying that she was doing it because she loved me so much she wanted to hurt me.'

Felix placed a hand on Asher's bare knee and squeezed gently, hoping it would help Asher feel more grounded.

'I couldn't move my body. I tried, but it wouldn't move. She just kept nipping me, all over.' He stopped to steady himself, trying to stifle the wracking sobs. 'She said that she loved me, but if she loved me, why would she do that?'

'Ash,' Felix said, his voice a low hum. 'Mummy would never hurt you. Ever. I promise you.'

'But she did,' Asher said.

'I know it felt that way, but Mummy loved you so much, she'd never hurt you.' Felix tore through his thoughts, trying to find an explanation for what happened last night.

'Maybe you were dreaming and you hurt yourself,' Felix said in desperation. It was the only explanation that made logical sense, and he was attempting to hold onto any semblance of logic.

'I didn't,' Asher said.

Felix shook his head. 'I know, I know. Bloody hell, Ash. What's happening to us?'

'It's *her*. It's Lilith, she did something to us.'

Sighing, Felix slowly nodded his head, 'I think you're right.'

'It wasn't Mummy,' Asher said, as though trying to convince himself of this fact.

'No, it wasn't. I promise you it wasn't.' For the first time as a parent, Felix felt utterly lost. He didn't know what to do. 'Can you show me all the bruises please?'

Asher nodded and stood from the chair. He peeled off his pyjama top and dropped it to the floor. Felix did everything in his power to keep his face blank. Inside, his body was alight. His stomach churned as he looked at the purpling bruises. They dotted across Asher's skin like a dalmatian's coat, not completely covering his skin, but marring the landscape sporadically. They lined his arms. And legs.

'We need to go to the doctor,' Felix said.

'No.' Asher picked up his shirt and pulled it back over his head.

'You need to go to the doctor,' Felix repeated.

'They're just bruises,' Asher said.

They'd fallen too readily into the headspace where whatever had happened to Asher had a supernatural origin, and that wasn't a safe place to reside. Before reverting to supernatural explanations, medical explanations needed to be explored. That's what a sane, sensible parent would do.

'We need to rule out if there's anything else going on,' Felix said. He'd once taught a kid that bruised easily, it turned out to be a symptom of leukaemia.

'They'll take me away from you,' Asher said.

Felix tipped his chin down to make eye contact with his son. 'What?' He was astonished by the words he'd just heard.

'They'll think you did it and they'll take me away from you. Rory's parents used to hit him. Mrs Robinson found the bruises and social services took him away from his mum and dad. He doesn't see them anymore.'

Felix was consistently surprised by how much his son knew about the world.

'But I didn't hurt you.'

'But how would I explain it? I went to sleep and woke up with bruises,' Asher said. 'If I tell them my dead mum did it, they'll lock me up and throw away the key.' Asher spoke with utter seriousness.

'Come here,' Felix said, holding Asher tightly against him. 'I'm sorry this is happening, but I will fix it, okay? I promise you. I will fix this.'

Felix felt Asher nod against his stomach.

'I'm going to ring Uncle Eli and see what he thinks, okay?'

'What about Nanna? She'll know what to do, right?' Asher said. Nanna was Felix and Eli's mother. She lived in an over-60s flat across town. After having a stroke a couple of years ago, she'd not been too steady on her feet. Both Felix and Eli had offered for her to live with them but she would have none of it. She wanted her own space, she said, and so she bought herself a little flat. Carers were always on hand if she needed anything, not that she ever did, but it gave Felix and Eli peace of mind. Telling his mother about what was happening was a last resort. The woman was very opinionated about anything resembling supernatural origins. She'd kill Felix for inviting Lilith into their home, just to prove that she was a phoney.

'Let's call Uncle Eli first,' Felix said.

'Because Nanna scares you,' Asher said.

'Damn right she does,' Felix said, smirking.

Felix brought Asher a glass of water and a bowl of cornflakes. Asher sat quietly and munched his breakfast while Felix called Eli.

'Morning,' Eli said. When he answered the video call request, he wiped a hand across his face.

'Were you asleep?' Felix said.

'I'm self-employed,' Eli said. 'Of course I was asleep.'

'Asher woke up covered in bruises. He said Jenna did it when he was asleep. That she nipped him over and over again.'

'What the fuck?' Eli said.

Asher snorted, milk coming out of his nose.

'Asher is next to me,' Felix said.

'Sorry Ash,' Eli said, his facial expression not changing from the mask of worry. 'Take me into a different room.'

Felix did as he was commanded and walked into the living room.

'Can Asher hear me?' Eli said.

'No,' Felix replied.

'You need to pull yourself together. What's happening to you?' Eli said.

'What?' Felix said, taken aback by the tone of Eli's words.

'What's happening to you? Take Asher to the hospital for god's sake.'

'He doesn't want to go.'

'He's a child. You're his dad. Make him go.'

'But how do I explain the bruises?' Felix said, a lump the size of a tennis ball in his throat.

'You don't. You let the doctors explain it. I'm coming round now.'

Eli hung up the phone, leaving Felix to stare at the blank screen.

Eli walked into the house without knocking, throwing his keys on the sideboard next to the front door. Specs launched himself through the house, searching for Asher, who he found sitting on the sofa in the front room. Asher's giggles filled the house. Chances were that Specs was licking Asher's face, which never failed to make Asher laugh.

Felix shouted from the kitchen, 'In here.'

Eli was greeted with a mug of coffee placed in front of his usual chair at the kitchen table. His brother's obvious attempt to get on his good side.

'Do you want to see the bruises?' Felix said.

'No, not yet. I'll look later, if Asher will let me. I'm worried about you.'

'I don't know what's happening…' Felix admitted, lowering his eyes to the table.

'You're not right. Not since Lilith. It's like you're not really here, you're living in a fantasy world.'

'You don't believe that something isn't right here?'

'No, I do. I do.' Eli nodded. 'You can't be raised by Mum and not believe in stuff like that, but sometimes there's an easier explanation, you know?'

'What's that?' Felix said.

'PTSD or something. This whole thing with Lilith has triggered you.'

'PTSD, that's your explanation? Felix's eyes darkened.

'Yes. Even if there is something supernatural going on, the way Lilith treated those people who'd lost loved ones has triggered something in you. It touched a nerve and you snapped.'

'You think I'm mental?' Felix said.

'No, I didn't say that. I think you need help. I think you need to talk to somebody. I think Asher does too.'

'A therapist? That's your solution.'

'It's part of the solution. You never saw a therapist after Jenna's death and you should have. You know you should have. You can't just get over something like that without help. And Asher, well, it's a lot for a kid to grow up without their mother.'

'I can't believe you,' Felix said.

'I'm trying to help. I'm trying to be practical,' Eli said.

Felix slammed his fist into the table. 'Fuck.'

'Felix,' Eli said in an attempt to comfort his brother. 'You need to talk to somebody.'

'I'd have to lie to them. If I tell them I see dead people, I'm sectioned. What's the point of therapy if I'm only going to tell them half-truths?'

'I'm going to go and look at the bruises,' Eli said. Felix was impossible to talk to when he was in one of his moods. It felt like he drained all the energy out of the air. He'd been the same since they were kids. Felix was a parent. An adult. It was his job to keep Asher safe and happy and, right now, Eli wasn't convinced Felix was up to the task. He regretted showing Felix the damn advert in the first place. He'd never anticipated it having a response like this. He thought it was funny, both from the standpoint of the terribly designed advert (a graphic designer's wet dream), and the fact that people actually paid for her shitty fake services. Until Felix had kicked off, Eli hadn't realised that the 'gullible' people were really 'desperate' people.

'Hi Ash,' he said, walking into the living room. Specs lay with Asher on the sofa, his big head in Asher's lap. The bruises were dark. Bile rose from Eli's stomach.

'Hi,' Asher replied.

'Can I see your bruises?' he asked.

'Sure,' Asher said. He gently pushed Specs off him and stood up.

'How did you get them?' Eli asked.

'Mummy did it when I was asleep,' he mumbled.

*What the hell was happening?*

# Reviewing Her Services

Eli hovered all day, even after Felix asked him if he had work to be doing. The work could wait, Eli assured him. Felix knew he was being babysat. The anger it made him feel was like pins and needles glancing across the surface of his skin. He didn't need a babysitter. He needed the weird shit to stop.

As a result of Eli's protestations, Felix booked an appointment with a family therapist. She was the best-rated therapist nearby, and so there was a waiting list. That suited Felix perfectly. It would get Eli off his back and allow him to fix whatever was happening in his house. All day he toyed with the idea of calling Lilith and forcing her to come back and rectify whatever damage she'd done. He'd all but concluded that Lilith was at fault for what was happening in his house.

It was about 5 pm when Felix's mobile rang. He, Eli, Asher, and Specs were laid across the sofas in the living room watching Parent Trap, Eli's film of choice (and the least scary film they had in their collection). The name Lilith Lavelle flashed onto the screen.

Felix flung himself off the sofa and walked into the kitchen. Without missing a beat, Eli untangled himself from Asher and followed.

'Hello,' Felix said into the phone.

'Hello Felix,' Lilith said.

'Speaker,' Eli mouthed to Felix, who rolled his eyes but acquiesced.

'I was just calling to check in with you. I noticed that you'd not left a review of my services yet and I wanted to ask if you'd maybe be able to take the time to do that.'

A laugh escaped Felix's mouth before he could hold it back.

'Is everything okay?' she asked.

Eli stared at Felix, observing him as you would a specimen in a lab.

'No, it's not.'

'I'm sorry?' Lilith said, she clearly hadn't been anticipating that response.

'What did you do?' Felix said, his voice barely more than a croak.

'Excuse me,' Lilith said.

'You did something to us,' he said.

'What are you talking about?'

'You did something. You did something to us. What did you do?' Felix said, the words pouring out of him like a tidal wave.

'Slow down, Felix. Tell me what happened.'

Felix did. He told her the truth of why he'd booked her services in the first place. He told her that he'd reported her to various bodies. He told her about all the creepy shit happening in his house. He told her everything, right up to Asher's bruises.

'You did something to us. Why?'

'I think it would be better if you didn't leave a review. Take your son to see a doctor.' Lilith said, after a beat.

The phone clicked off. The connection was lost.

Felix looked to Eli, blinking wildly.

'Call her back. Tell her you need her to fix it,' Eli said.

Felix tapped the call button next to her name. 'The person you are trying to call is unreachable.'

'She's blocked my number,' Felix said. A hot flush swarmed his body. He dropped into a chair. His elbows found his knees, and his fingers found his hair.

'What the fuck have I done?' Felix said.

'I don't know. I don't know,' Eli said. He pulled out a chair and sat across from Felix, placing his hands on his brother's shoulders. 'We'll get through this, okay. We will. I promise.'

# Brother or Babysitter?

'Can you stay here tonight Uncle Eli?' Asher asked. Eli noticed Felix's body language change after the phone call with Lilith. A tightly wound bundle of nerves, ready to explode. He was glad Asher had asked, because it saved him broaching the subject with his brother. Felix didn't like accepting help. It was one of his more annoying traits.

'I can, Ash, if you want,' Eli said, looking to Felix for confirmation. Felix nodded and mouthed 'thank you'.

Asher visibly relaxed after Eli said he would sleep over. When the sky darkened, and Specs realised that they were sleeping over, he wandered over to the back door to be let out.

'I'll do it,' Asher said, opening the back door and allowing Specs to venture into the garden to do his business.

Asher stood leaning against the doorframe. He seemed so much older than his twelve years. Whatever had happened here the last few days had aged him. He was no longer an innocent kid.

'I think we need to set up some cameras,' Felix said.

'You're going full-blown *Paranormal Activity* on me?' Eli said, trying to joke.

'It was the only part of the movie that made sense. I feel like I'm going crazy, Eli. All this shit is happening and then the next day I wonder whether I was dreaming. Whether I made it up. I need to see concrete proof that I'm not crazy.'

'You're not crazy,' Eli said. He wished his voice sounded more convincing.

'I'm going to go and pick up some cameras to set up around the house. Stay here with Asher, okay?'

'Fine, whatever,' Eli said. There was zero point arguing with Felix when he'd set his mind on something.

Specs galloped back into the house and Asher shut the door.

'I'm just nipping out, Ash. I'll be back soon,' Felix said.

Asher nodded. He'd heard their whole conversation anyway.

'Come on Ash, we'll watch some TV until he gets back,' Eli said. They walked together into the living room, Specs close on their heels.

Eli sat on the sofa and Asher sat close by him, Specs jumping up and laying across Asher's feet. Asher leaned his head against his uncle's shoulder. Shifting slightly, Eli wrapped his arm around Asher and pulled him closer. Asher hadn't been particularly cuddly since he'd hit his tween years.

'Everything okay?' Eli asked. They both kept their eyes fixed on the TV.

'I'm scared,' Asher said.

'What do you think's happening?' Eli said.

'Our house is haunted.'

Eli pushed down a phrase he'd heard somewhere, *houses aren't haunted, people are*. That particular nugget of information wasn't especially helpful. Eli nodded and tightened his grip on Asher.

'I won't let anything hurt you. Neither would your dad. You know that, right? We'll keep you safe.'

'Something hurt me last night,' Asher said. His voice had a robotic quality to it. He was right. Felix hadn't kept Asher safe last night.

'I'm here now. So is Specs. Do you really think Specs would let anything hurt you?'

On cue, Specs yawned a big Staffy yawn and snuggled deeper into Asher's legs.

Asher gave Specs's head a rub and laughed. 'Yeah, Specs will keep me safe.'

'He will. Those teeth aren't just for show,' Eli said. 'I mean, how else is he going to eat treats and ghosts?'

Asher laughed again, and Eli felt like he was winning.

They lay and watched TV in silence, snuggled against one another, until Felix came home with bags filled with tech gear.

'You guys want to help me set this stuff up?' he asked.

'Not really,' Asher mumbled.

Eli held back a laugh and untangled himself from his nephew. 'Let's see what you've got.'

Felix unpacked the bags on the kitchen table. Eli watched as Felix pulled camera after camera out of the bag. 'How much did you spend?'

'You sound like mum.' Felix rolled his eyes.

'It's a valid question,' Eli said.

'I spent a fair amount,' Felix admitted. 'There's one for the bottom of the stairs, where I saw the shadow figures. One for the landing at the top of the stairs. One for my room, and one for Asher's. I've also got one for the kitchen and the living room, just to be safe.'

'We'd better get to work then.'

Each camera took about twenty minutes to set up and connect to the internet. Felix had bought ones that started recording when there was movement. The recording would be saved to the Cloud for him to watch later.

As Felix was making the final adjustments to the kitchen camera, and Eli was packing away the box from Asher's bedroom camera, Specs gave a single bark so loud that Eli dropped the camera's box and ran downstairs. Asher and Specs were still on the sofa but the dog was staring intently into the corner of the room, a low rumbling growl leaking from his mouth.

'What is it, Specs?' Asher said. He sat upright, staring in the same spot as Specs.

Another earth-shaking bark. Eli hadn't realised Specs could bark like that.

'Specs,' Eli said, edging toward the dog.

Felix stood next to Eli, and placed a hand on his arm. 'Wait,' Felix whispered.

The growl stretched on.

'Can you smell that?' Felix said.

'Perfume?' Eli said. It made no sense.

'Jenna's perfume. I smelt it last night too.'

'But you don't see her,' Eli said.

'No.'

'What does that mean?' Eli didn't dare tear his eyes away from the spot Specs continued to growl at to look at his brother.

'I don't know. I'm certain it's not her, though. If it was Jenna, I'm sure I'd be able to see her. Just like the others. This feels wrong.'

'Wrong?'

'Bad. Evil. Sick. Whatever you want to call it. This isn't a spirit. This is something dark, and it's messing with us.'

'Why though?' Eli said.

'It has something to do with Lilith Lavelle. It all started with her.'

# Big Brother's Watching You

Although nothing had changed, Felix felt better knowing that the cameras would record anything *untoward.* Eli slept on the sofa downstairs. Specs slept at the bottom of Asher's bed. Felix attempted to sleep in his own bed. Sleep was an impossibility, all of his failings as a father kept whirling around inside his head like angry wasps trapped in a jar. Until last week, he felt like he'd done a pretty damn good job of raising Asher, and then he'd invited Lilith into their life and fucked everything up. Why couldn't he leave it alone? A headache drilled into the back of his skull. Paracetamol hadn't touched it, not even the extra strength ones you had to get over the counter at the chemist.

When the walls started to bleed, Felix thought he was dreaming. The cliché wasn't lost on him, even through the moment of sheer terror. The walls not only bled, but breathed. They expanded and contracted. A heartbeat echoed through his bedroom. The blood was thick, syrupy, slow to run. It started at the ceiling and lazily dribbled down each of the walls, building in puddles on the floor. The room filled with the sickly smell of iron. Felix choked, the stench cloying at his throat. He had to stand. He had to get to his son.

'Asher,' he said. His legs were unsteady, the floor moving like a funhouse, shifting this way and that. Felix stumbled to his door and flung it open. The hallway mirrored his bedroom perfectly. The blood. The heartbeat. The breathing. On he stumbled, toward Asher's room.

'Eli!' he shouted, but his voice didn't carry. It spluttered, barely audible. 'Eli!' he tried again. Frustration clawed at him, sinking its fangs into his neck.

The door to Asher's room remained firmly closed when Felix flung himself into it. He turned the handle and tried again. Nothing. It stuck fast.

'Asher! Eli!' he called in desperation.

Felix slammed his shoulder against the door.

Specs's crazed barks sounded from the other side.

'Specs.' Felix breathed the dog's name like a prayer.

The floors became slick with blood. The house began to shake, not the expanding and contracting of breathing, but violently shaking. Trembling. The heartbeat quickened, then stopped dead.

Specs's barks grew to a frenzy.

Felix continued to throw himself into the door.

'Open, open,' he muttered. 'God, please open.'

The sound of glass smashing echoed around Felix. Asher's voice cut through the cacophony.

'What's happening? Help! Daddy! Uncle Eli!'

Specs added to the deafening noise. Glass that Felix couldn't see continued to smash. The sound of metal dinting and bending reverberated around him. Sounds he'd never heard firsthand, but that Jenna would have. A car accident.

'ELI!' Felix yelled.

His brother rounded the top of the stairs. He lost his footing on a pool of blood, skidding into the wall.

'What the fuck?' Eli said, panting heavily.

'Help me get this door open!'

They didn't need to speak. Together, they launched themselves against the door, slamming so hard that it shook in the frame. It didn't budge.

Asher screamed, sending ice down Felix's spine. Specs's barking reached fever pitch. The sounds of a car accident. The house shaking. It was too much. Felix's mind felt like it would snap.

Screams pierced their ears. Shrieks of agony. Felix recognised the screams, he'd heard them when Asher came bloody and crying into the world. Jenna. Jenna's wails filled the gaps in the noise.

Together, they threw themselves at the door again.

The screams. The blood. The shaking. The metal, and glass, and dog barking.

They hit the door again.

And again.

And again.

It flew open, bouncing off the wall and back towards them. Felix barrelled into the room, pushing past Eli. In that moment, he didn't care about Eli. Asher was all he could think of. The relief at the door finally releasing was short-lived when he saw Asher curled in a foetal position, rocking on the floor. Specs stood guard in front of him, barking and snarling in various directions. The threat was all around them.

Specs ceased barking when he saw Eli and Felix enter the room. Instead, he whined. A high-pitched, desperate sound. The house didn't stop convulsing. The blood didn't stop dripping. Sounds of a car crash, of crushing metal, and Jenna's desperate screams filled the space.

'Asher,' Felix said, kneeling in front of his son, the blood warm against his knees.

Eli was at his side. 'Asher,' he said.

'Hey,' Felix gently pulled on Asher's arms, attempting to coax him to unfurl.

'No, no, please make it stop,' Asher said, his voice almost drowned out by the sounds of crushing metal and breaking glass. Noises that echoed Jenna's final moments.

'Asher,' Felix shouted. He could barely hear anything over his own heartbeat thrumming in his ears.

'She's dying, she's dying,' he cried. 'Mummy's dying.'

Jenna's wailing intensified. Felix reached to cover his ears; Eli and Asher did the same. Specs shrunk and continued to cry. The screaming ended with a single deafening screech. The house breathed a sigh of relief and all traces of blood vanished.

Felix blinked rapidly. How had everything changed so quickly?

'She died. Mummy died. I saw it. I felt it.'

Asher's little body shook with heaving sobs. Felix rubbed Asher's back, and tried to catch his own breath. He watched as Eli slowly climbed to his feet, raking his fingers through his hair, cutting deep gouges in the blonde mop.

'Now do you believe me?' Felix said. He couldn't stop his body from spasming, the result of too much adrenaline running through his system.

'We need to get out of here. Now,' Eli said. 'I'll pack Asher a bag.'

Felix remained on the floor with Asher while Eli ran around the room filling up his school backpack with clothes and toys. Whispering to Asher did nothing to soothe him. In the end, Felix heaved Asher into his arms, carrying him like a baby. They walked to the car in silence, Specs walking as close to Eli as physically possible.

As they climbed into the car, Specs turned and growled once more at the house. That was all the sign that Felix needed that the house was fifty shades of fucked up, as Jenna would have said. The irony that he needed a genuine spiritual cleansing, or whatever the hell you did when your house was haunted, wasn't lost on Felix. But, as far as he knew, only frauds and con artists plied these services, so he was shit out of luck.

# The Jump Scare

Felix slept fitfully at Eli's house. Asher had his own bedroom there, for when he had sleepovers with his uncle or, more accurately, sleepovers with Specs, but it was a single bed and so he and Asher were cramped together. Specs slept on the floor beside the bed. A thin layer of sweat slicked Felix's skin. While he didn't feel calm, by any stretch of the imagination, he felt a damn sight better than he had done at home.

Felix woke the next morning without an alarm. He unwound his arm from underneath Asher and slid out of the bed. Specs's eyes followed Felix to the door. The dog didn't bother to move his head. When Felix left the room, Specs shut his eyes once more and immediately started snoring.

Eli's bedroom door creaked open as Felix attempted to creep by.

'Morning,' Eli said. Heavy bags littered the skin under his eyes.

'Did last night actually happen?' Felix said, forgoing the *good morning*. 'Like, really happen?'

Eli nodded. 'We need to watch the recordings,' he said.

'I feel like I'm going mad,' Felix said, folding his arms over his chest.

'You're not the only one,' Eli said.

They sat together at Eli's breakfast bar, steaming cups of coffee before each of them. Eli opened his laptop and passed it over to Felix to log into his Cloud server. Several recorded files popped up.

'It caught something,' Felix said.

'Could just have been us moving around though,' Eli said.

Felix nodded. He wasn't sure what the best-case scenario was: that the cameras had picked up malevolent activity, or that they hadn't. In the first instance, they were being terrorised by something paranormal. In the second, they were in some kind of folie a trois (there was one too many people for a folie a deux). Paranormal entity vs mental illness. Both options sucked.

'Ready?' Felix asked, the cursor hovering over the first video file.

'Go on,' Eli said.

Felix clicked the video. It was from the camera named 'Landing'. It covered the whole hallway at the top of the stairs. The air vanished from Felix's lungs as he watched his bedroom door fly open. He looked drunk. He swayed along the hallway, stumbling and steadying himself on the walls. The cameras didn't pick up audio, an oversight that Felix felt in the pit of his stomach.

There was no blood. The walls looked perfectly normal. Felix watched himself wrestle with the door. Eventually, Eli came from off-camera to aid him. After numerous attempts, the door opened and the camera switched off.

'Next,' Felix said, the word sounding more like a grunt. He clicked on the next recording. It was from the living room camera. It showed Eli jerking awake and throwing himself off the sofa. He ran out of the room. The camera cut to black.

Felix clicked the next recording without a sound. The camera was labelled 'Bottom of Stairs'. It showed Eli barrelling out of the living room and toward the stairs. He was in and out of the frame in seconds.

The next recording was labelled 'Asher's Room'. The camera was placed just above Asher's doorway, angled down to get a full view of the room. Specs paced around the room while Asher slept in bed. Specs looked to be whining, his mouth opening and closing slightly. Asher sat bolt upright, looking at Specs. The dog morphed into full angry barks. They were directed in all corners of the room.

Asher turned to look at the wall behind him. Shock peeled across his face. He began to scream a silent scream that tore at Felix's insides. He climbed slowly out of bed, his eyes darting all around his bedroom. He was talking, shouting, asking for his dad to come and rescue him. Fingernails dug into the fleshy part of Felix's hand as he tried to hold back burning tears. Asher dropped to the floor and wound his arms around his knees. Specs continued barking, spit flying from his enraged muzzle.

In the video, Asher's bedroom door opened. Felix and Eli burst in. Felix knelt beside his son and tried to comfort him. Eli hovered over them, before turning his attention to Specs.

'What the fuck?' Felix said. He leaned closer to the laptop screen. He tapped the spacebar to pause the video. Ice pierced his brain. He tried to find the words to explain what he was seeing.

'Oh my god,' Eli said. 'Is that Jenna?'

In the corner of the room, a warped version of Jenna stood. She stooped down over them, so tall that her neck bent at the ceiling. Her arms trailed to the floor. Her face twisted, moving slowly toward the crumpled mess of Felix and Asher. A Cheshire Cat smile slashed across her face. Teeth protruded from her mouth. She turned to look at the camera and opened her mouth to scream. Jenna's sickening face swooped towards the camera. Both Eli and Felix jumped backwards instinctively.

The screen went black.

Felix stared at the blank screen, attempting to wrangle his thoughts and emotions into some kind of cohesive feeling. He could feel Eli's eyes drilling holes into him. He couldn't force himself to look at his brother.

'I need a minute,' Felix said. He walked out of the backdoor and into the garden without looking back.

The summer drizzle quickly coated his skin.

'Here,' Eli said. Felix hadn't realised his brother had joined him outside. He held out a packet of Marlboros. Felix took one without a second thought. He hadn't smoked for over ten years. He'd stopped when Jenna was pregnant with Asher, and started again when she died. The last bout of smoking only lasted a few months before he kicked the habit again.

Felix held the cigarette to his mouth, Eli brought the lighter to touch the tip. He inhaled deeply, feeling the smoke coat the inside of his mouth. It was difficult to remember why he'd given up.

'Thought you didn't smoke anymore,' Felix said, after exhaling a stream of white smoke.

'In case of emergencies,' Eli said. Felix noticed his brother hadn't taken a cigarette out of the pack.

'I don't know what to do,' Felix said. He sunk to the ground and sat on the cold, wet concrete step.

'You need to talk to Mum,' Eli said.

'I know,' Felix said. Even as an adult, he was still scared to death of his mother's wrath. She'd all but kill him for putting Asher in danger. To be fair, she couldn't make Felix feel worse about the situation than he already did. He just hated disappointing her, especially in her old age. She was frailer than she'd admit.

'I think you should send the videos to Lilith. The last one at least. She needs to see this. Maybe she can help. If she did this, she might be able to undo it.'

'Eli,' Felix warned.

'She did something. It all started with her. She knows something. You *have* to show her the proof. Maybe that's what it takes to get her back here.'

'I don't want to see that bitch ever again,' Felix said. He'd never once called a woman a bitch in his life, the word felt like acid on his tongue.

'If she can get this to stop, it's worth it.'

'Fuck,' Felix said. He dropped the cigarette onto the floor and slunk back inside. He needed to send the video to Lilith now before he changed his mind.

He tapped her email address, attached the video, and wrote, *'This is what you did. You need to fix it.'*

'Done,' he said to Eli, who hovered behind him.

'Good. Now we wait.'

# Online Friends

Lilith's response was almost immediate.

*Dear Mr Eastwood,*

*Please do not contact me again. I will be forced to take legal action if you continue to attempt to besmirch my name. What you're claiming is happening to you has nothing to do with me, and I would advise that you seek psychological treatment. If you contact me again, I will have no choice but to take this matter further with my solicitor.*

*Regards,*

*Lilith Lavelle*

'Wow,' Felix said. 'I mean, that's pretty much what I expected, but-'

'It's the fact that she gave you the old *regards* trick. That's so funny. There are no *kind regards* from her, only *regards*. She hates you.' Eli laughed into his coffee mug.

'I'm glad you're able to find the humour in this,' Felix said.

'Look, nothing's happened since you came here, at least. As far as I'm concerned, you guys are safe now. The haunting, or whatever it is, is happening at your house.'

'The house that I'm mortgaged up to the eyeballs on,' Felix said. 'How the hell do you sell a haunted house?'

'I think there's a book about that,' Eli said. 'Grady Hendrix? That sounds right.'

'Since when do you read?' Felix said.

'I don't,' Eli said, a sly smile crawling across his face.

'Some guy you're seeing?'

'I'm not one to kiss and tell.' Eli shrugged.

'I'm presuming the book is a work of fiction?' Felix said.

'Of course it fucking is,' Eli said, laughing. 'There are no how-to guides about selling a haunted house.'

Despite himself, Felix laughed. The whole situation he'd found himself in was not only unbelievable, but absolutely ridiculous.

'If somebody told me this was happening to them, I'd send them straight to a therapist. I'd think they were delusional.'

'I know,' Eli said. He shook his head.

'I want to know more about this guy you're dating later, though. Don't think you got away with it that easily.'

'We'll see,' Eli said. 'More coffee?'

'Nice segue,' Felix said. 'Yeah, I'm going to check on Ash. I hear movement.'

Asher had been out like a light the second his head hit the pillow, which was a blessing. He needed sleep after the night they'd had. *Kids are resilient,* Felix kept reminding himself as he walked up the stairs to Asher's room. *He'll be fine.* Felix wasn't naïve enough to think that the aftermath of the haunting would stop just because they'd left their home. And, even if it had, which Felix didn't dare to allow himself to hope for, there was still the issue of what to do with the house. Eli would let them live with him as long as they wanted, he knew that, but could Felix, in good conscience, sell their home knowing what happened there? Probably not.

Once he'd reached the top step, he squeezed his eyes shut and steadied his breathing. Everything would be okay, they'd figure it out.

'Specs?' Felix said.

The dog was outside Asher's room. Hackles raised, a groaning noise escaping from him. He sniffed at the bottom of the door, pawing at it.

'What's going on Specs?' Felix said. There was no reason for Asher to shut the dog out of the room. They were inseparable.

Felix knocked on the door before opening it. He'd read in a parenting book at some point that it was important to give your children privacy, especially when they're becoming teenagers. He remembered what he'd been like as a teenager, how many close calls there had been when his mother came home unexpectedly, he never wanted his son to experience that.

When Asher didn't answer, Felix opened the door a crack and peered inside. Specs forced the door the rest of the way, careening into the room on his little legs. Asher was sitting in bed, laptop on his knees, staring at the screen.

'Asher? Everything okay?' Felix said.

Asher's eyes never left the screen. His fingers moved across the keys.

'Ash?' Felix said, edging closer. 'What are you doing?'

Asher didn't respond. He continued typing. Specs jumped onto the bed beside Asher and restarted his whining. Specs's snout sneaked closer to Asher's face. The whining intensified. The dog's tongue lapped against Asher's cheek. Still no response.

Felix strode over to the bed and pulled the laptop out of Asher's grip.

'Oy!' Asher snarled, snapping out of his trance.

'I was talking to you,' Felix said.

'I didn't hear you,' Asher mumbled.

Felix placed the laptop on top of the dresser, his eyes caught the open Word Document. Asher had been writing, filling the page with words that didn't make sense.

*I'm here for you.*

*Mummy?*

*Yes, it's me.*

*Why did you hurt me?*

*I did it because I love you. I needed you to understand that I was real.*

*But it hurt.*

*Asher, darling. I would never do anything to hurt you if I didn't have to.*

Felix's hands found the dresser top. He braced himself to prevent him from collapsing in a puddle on the floor.

'What is this?' Felix whirled around to look at Asher. All of the colour had vanished from his face.

'I was talking to Mummy,' he said. Each word was forced, like his throat closed around them, trying to keep them inside.

'You think this is your mum?' Felix said.

'Yes. It is. She told me it is.'

'That is not your mum, Asher, for god's sake. How many times do I have to tell you that? Your mum isn't here. I would see her if she was. Whatever this is,' Felix gestured wildly to the laptop. 'It isn't your mum. It isn't.'

'It is!' Asher's brows furrowed deep into his forehead, his teeth gritted together.

'Asher, it isn't.'

'She said you'd do this. She said you'd try to keep her from me. I hate you.'

Felix saw only red. He rushed to the bed and grabbed Asher by the shoulders. Their noses were inches apart.

'That isn't your mum. She's dead. She's gone. You need to understand that.' He shook his son, praying desperately that his words would get through, that Asher would understand.

'Stop lying!' Asher screamed. Felix flinched backward, landing at the bottom of the bed.

'Hey, what's happening,' Eli said, surveying the scene.

'He thinks he's talking to Jenna,' Felix said. 'Through the laptop.'

'Oh,' Eli said.

'I am! I am talking to her.' Asher's hands balled into fists on top of the duvet.

'Asher,' Felix said.

'It is her,' Asher said.

'Mind if I look?' Eli said.

Asher shrugged. Colour filled his cheeks.

Eli approached the laptop. He stood in silence for a few minutes, scrolling through the document.

'Jesus Christ,' Eli said, under his breath. 'How much did you read?'

'Not much, why?' Felix said. He looked to Asher who hung his head and stared into his lap.

'Come here,' Eli said to Felix.

Eli pointed a finger at the screen.

*Daddy isn't safe. He doesn't love you. You need to come to me.*

*Daddy loves me.*

*Not as much as I do. I'm your mother. There's nothing like a mother's love.*

*I don't want to leave Daddy.*

*Sometimes you have to do things you don't want to.*

*Can't we all live together?*

*No.*

*Why?*

*Because Daddy isn't dead. If you want Mummy, you need to*

The last sentence ended abruptly. Felix put his head in his hands, massaging the bridge of his nose.

'Asher, I'm sorry,' Felix said. He walked over to the bed and pulled Asher against his chest. At first, Asher remained still. Eventually, he relaxed into his father's arms and began to sob. Felix stroked Asher's hair, holding him as close as he could. 'I'm sorry for shouting at you. I'm so sorry.'

Felix had failed his son. There was nothing he was more certain of. He'd always thought Asher had been fine. Jenna died when Asher was very young. He'd hoped that would make it easier for Asher to cope. He hadn't realised how much Asher still yearned for her. He should have known better. He should have paid more attention.

Eli sat at the bottom of the bed. Felix felt the mattress dip under his weight. Specs began to nuzzle between Asher and Felix, wanting to get in on the action.

'Dumb dog,' Eli said, his voice filled with love.

'Hey,' Felix said, separating from Asher so that Specs could lick away Asher's tears.

Felix looked at Eli and shook his head. The message was clear: '*What the fuck are we going to do?*

# Never Too Old

'You have to,' Eli said.

'I know.' Felix tipped his head back and looked at the artexed ceiling.

'You have to do it now,' Eli said.

'I know.'

Felix did not want to go and see his mother. It was the last thing he wanted to do. Actually, that wasn't quite the truth. The last thing he wanted to do was to go home to a haunted house.

'Go now,' Eli said.

Felix glanced towards the sofa, at Asher and Specs huddled together. Asher slept, wrapped in a grey fleecy blanket. Grey, like most things in Eli's house.

'He'll be fine. I won't let him out of my sight.'

'Fine,' Felix said. 'Fine.'

'You have to do this. Mum will know what to do, she always does.'

Felix nodded, knowing Eli was right. Felix was able to see spirits, but his mother could do so much more than that. She didn't block them out, like Felix did, pretending he didn't see them every day. His mum welcomed them in. She could *feel* them, their energy, what they needed. She helped them. A real-life *Ghost Whisperer,* the brothers used to joke. Melinda Gordon had nothing on Clara Eastwood.

It was only a short drive to Whistling Hills, the over 60's apartment complex. It sat nestled in the outskirts of the town, surrounded by hillsides and pavements that seemed to be consistently slick with rain. The building was an interesting dichotomy, it smelled like death, but was full of life. The air was stale, heavy with the unique smell associated with the last phase of life. Like dust and food and something darker. But Felix's mum loved it there. There were always people walking around the corridors, albeit slowly and carefully, talking and laughing. Most of the residents went down to the communal dining hall for at least one of their meals each day. They also had singers and entertainers on every Friday evening. His mum was happy there, and Felix was about to ruin her day.

His mum's room was at the end of a long corridor. She'd insisted that the door be painted lavender, a colour that she said warded off evil. He'd always thought that she was joking, but now Felix caught himself wondering whether he should have painted his own door lavender prior to Lilith's arrival. He knocked twice and walked into the small foyer area. She always left the door unlocked throughout the day.

'Mum?' he said. There were three doorways off the foyer. A bathroom, a bedroom, and a living area. All of them were closed.

'Mum?' he said again, opening the door to the living room a crack. The kitchenette and living room were empty. Felix's mum was at the age now where this made him panic.

Leaving the living room door open, he knocked on the bathroom door and opened it tentatively. Nothing.

*Maybe she's just napping,* Felix thought, but why wasn't she answering?

He opened the bedroom door, looked inside, and immediately closed the door tightly. Heat flooded his face. His mother had been obscured by the grey-haired man lying precariously atop her.

'Mum?' Felix shouted through the now-closed door.

'One minute,' his mum said. Her voice was muffled, presumably by the man on top of her.

Felix walked into the living room and sat on the sofa. He put his head into his hands. 'What the fuck?' he whispered. He shook his head, not knowing whether to laugh or cry. Felix stared at the clock on the mantlepiece and waited for his mum to join him.

Ten minutes later. He heard the front door open and close. His mum shuffled into the living room. Her face was almost as flushed as his was. She walked over to the kitchen.

'Do you want a cup of tea?'

'Are we not going to talk about-' Felix said.

'Do you want a cup of tea?' his mum repeated.

'Have you washed your hands?' Felix said.

'Don't be so crude,' she said.

'I'm not the one rolling around in bed, with the door unlocked, at this time on a morning.'

The clock read 10.23.

'I've been up since six,' she said, putting tea bags into mugs and clicking on the kettle. 'And you usually let me know you're coming.'

She did have a point. Felix usually messaged her before he came to see her. He certainly wouldn't make that mistake again.

'I need to ask your advice about something,' Felix said. He'd put all thoughts about his mum's extracurricular activities to the back of his mind, for now.

'Okay,' she said. She placed the drinks on the coffee table and took a seat in her usual chair, a mechanical recliner that looked like it was made out of carpet.

'I did something really stupid,' he said.

His mum nodded. 'Tell me.'

Felix told her the truth. He told her absolutely everything. His mum didn't interrupt. She sat patiently while Felix told the story as best he could. As he spoke, a lump in his throat developed. His mum's face grew more stern, the wrinkles in her face becoming more pronounced as she frowned. She bit down on her lip, hard, a small trickle of blood oozing from the wound.

'What have you done?' she said when Felix finished. 'You stupid, stupid boy. What were you thinking?' Her eyes were wild.

'I thought I could help other people.'

'No, you wanted to be a saviour, that's different. You invited it in. You brought something into your home: something powerful to manifest like that. I dread to think what it is.'

'What do I do?' Felix asked. Any hope he had rested on his mum's shoulders. She knew more than anybody about life after death, about spirituality and the paranormal.

'I don't know,' she said.

Felix's heart fell into his stomach.

'You've put Asher and Eli at risk too. I can't believe you were so stupid. You don't mess with this kind of thing. It's common sense. I can barely look at you.' The words were forced through gritted teeth. Her eyes fixed on the mug in her hands.

'I need you to tell me what to do,' Felix said. 'I have no idea where to start.'

His mum began to mutter. He could barely hear her. 'Hail Mary, Full of Grace, The Lord is with thee. Blessed art thou among women, and blessed is the fruit of thy womb, Jesus. Holy Mary, Mother of God, pray for us sinners now, and at the hour of our death.'

'What are you doing?' he asked. As far as he knew, she wasn't Catholic. She was a proud agnostic.

'It's the next best thing. I believe in *something*, I just don't know what. And, right now, you need all the help you can get.'

She repeated the prayer again. Felix sat in silence and waited for her to finish.

'I've come across something like this before. A long time ago, when I was a teenager. But there's no guarantee this is the same thing.' She spoke as though in a dream. Her words trailed together. She didn't expect an answer.

'You have two options, as far as I know,' she said. She tore her eyes away from her tea to look at Felix. He could see the grief, the disappointment, in her eyes. 'You could do an exorcism, but it only works if you truly believe in Christ, and if you can find a priest willing to do it. Exorcisms don't work on non-believers, and the chances that you'll find somebody willing to conduct the exorcism is non-existent.'

'So that rules that out,' Felix said. 'What's my other option?'

'Kill the entity.'

'How do I do that?' Felix leaned over his knees toward his mother.

She closed her eyes. The muscles in her jaw tensed. She was remembering something, something bad.

'When the entity possesses a person, you have to kill the person. They can't be killed unless they're in a physical, and therefore vulnerable, body.'

# Psychic Gone AWOL

'You're not telling me I actually have to murder somebody,' Felix said. There was no way in his mind that he'd heard his mum correctly.

'Yes. Contrary to what films and books usually tell us, entities don't just mess around with the living for entertainment. They're not bored, they want something. If a being is so powerful that it can manipulate the environment in the way that this one did, why would it choose you? What entertainment would they get out of you, that they wouldn't get out of world leaders or members of the Church? It's chosen you for a reason. I dread to think what that reason might be.'

'So you're telling me to wait until it possesses somebody and then kill it?' Felix had to be sure he'd understood her correctly.

'That's what I'm saying.' Disappointment moulded her features like clay. Felix had never seen her look at him in such a way. Ever.

'How do you know this?' he asked.

'That's a story for another time,' she said. She paused, took a long gulp of her drink. 'I can't believe you were so stupid.' Her words broke Felix's heart.

'I didn't do it on purpose,' he said, a scorned child.

'You didn't *think*, Felix. And when you have a child, you always have to think.'

'There's no alternative?'

'Unless you and your son can convince yourselves to believe in some higher power quickly, there's no other way.'

'And you won't tell me how you know all this?' Felix wanted to bang his head against the wall. He felt like he'd just walked into the Twilight Zone.

'Not right now.'

'There's nobody who can help me?'

'You have to help yourself. There's nobody left to help you.' His mum had always been one for cryptic answers and riddles.

'There's something you're not telling me,' he said.

'I've told you everything you need to know. The rest of the story is fluff and filler. For another time, Felix. Now is not that time. You have to go back to Asher and Eli. You let it in. You have to see this through until the end. There is no other way.'

'I wish you'd just tell me how you know this,' he said. His tone was harsher than he would have liked, but talking around in circles was infuriating. 'You know what it is? Why can't you help us? I thought you'd be begging to come back with me.'

'Felix, don't be so stupid. I'm an old woman. What good could I do?'

Felix shook his head. His mum knew something. She *knew* something. It made no sense that she'd withhold information at that moment.

Felix didn't bother to hide the disappointment on his face. He'd come to his mum for information. She was the only person he knew that wasn't a fraud. He got his gift from her. Frustration clawed at his back as he left the room.

'Felix?' she said as his hand reached for the doorknob.

'What?' He turned to look at her. She looked as drained as he felt.

'Names are powerful. Find out its name.'

Felix returned to Eli's house with his tail between his legs. His mother's cryptic clues had done nothing to help. If anything, they'd made him feel a million times worse. Which was fair enough. This situation was mostly his fault, after all. His and Lilith's.

'She said that I needed to find out its name.' Felix filled Eli in on the conversation with their mother while Asher snuggled in a blanket, with Specs, and watched a movie in the living room.

'What the fuck does that mean?' Eli said.

'I have no idea,' Felix said.

'And you didn't think to ask?'

'Of course I did. She just shook her head at me and so I left.'

'She's being weird,' Eli said.

'No shit.' Felix massaged his temples.

'But she said that you'd '*invited* it *in*' and that you needed to find out *its* name. So she believes that this is being caused by an *it*, something that's beyond what we could possibly know about.'

Felix nodded.

'So why wouldn't she tell us what *it* was?'

'I don't know. I really don't know.'

'I'm going to call her,' Eli said. 'See if I can get more sense out of her.'

'Thank you,' Felix said.

'You need to call Lilith again,' Eli said.

'I know,' Felix said.

'I'll speak to Mum, you do that.'

Eli grabbed his phone from the kitchen counter and walked out of the room, leaving Felix alone. Muffled voices came from the TV. Felix poked his head into the living room.

Asher looked up from the pile of blankets. Specs didn't bother to move.

'Everything okay?' Felix said.

'Yes,' Asher said. The smile he gave didn't reach his eyes.

'I'll fix this, I promise,' he said.

'I know,' Asher said, laying his head back down and turning his attention back to the TV.

Slipping back into the kitchen, Felix found Lilith's number and dialled it from the house phone, an ancient relic his brother insisted on keeping, *just in case*.

He counted each ring. All seven of them. The answering machine kicked in.

'Hello, you've reached Lilith Lavelle Psychic Cleansing Services. Please leave your message after the tone, and I'll get back to you as soon as possible.'

'Lilith, it's Felix Eastwood. I really need to talk to you. You need to fix this. I'm desperate. You brought something into my house. It's messing with my son. It hurt him. Lilith, I need you to fix this. If you have any decency, you'll do the right thing. It's got worse. Asher is talking to what he thinks is his dead mother. He's just a kid. Please Lilith, he's just a kid.'

His hands shook as he ended the call. He squeezed the phone tightly in his fist, pressing the sharp edge to his forehead. Releasing it, he watched as it clattered to the table. He didn't say enough. He needed to do more. More to convince her that he needed her help. That he was telling the truth. He picked up the phone again, and with trembling fingers, called Lilith again.

Two rings. And then the voicemail.

'Lilith, the email I sent was… abrupt, I know. I'm terrified. I'm desperate. Whatever is happening to us isn't right. It's not, it's not right. I need to make it stop. My only job is to keep my son safe, and I've failed him. I've failed him by inviting you into our lives. Maybe this is happening to you too. Maybe you didn't do this to us on purpose, but I need your help. You're the only one who can help. I, I lied to you. When I invited you to our house I wanted to prove that you were a fraud, but there was more to it than that. I have a gift, my mother has the same gift. We can see the dead. We see those who have not yet passed into the next plane of existence, or whatever you want to call it. I believe in the paranormal, I do, because it's my life. I live this every day. I went to see my mother in her nursing home and she told me that the only way to save Asher was to wait for the demon, or the entity, whatever the fuck it is, to kill it. To do that, I'm supposed to wait for it to possess somebody and kill the vessel. There's more she's not telling me, but you might know. You *have* to know, right? Please, Lilith, please help.'

Felix hung up the phone again. Panic flooded his system. He was terrified. On some level, he'd thought that his mum might have a magic spell to bail him out. Or, failing that, Lilith would do the decent thing. But now he felt alone. So completely and utterly alone.

The door creaked open and Asher stood there.

'Dad?'

Felix looked up at his son, tears clouding his vision.

Asher padded across the room and sat on Felix's knee, in a way he'd not done since he was a child, and wrapped his arms around his neck. Felix breathed in the smell of his son.

'I'm sorry, Ash. I'm so sorry.'

'It's okay, Dad. It'll be okay. Don't cry.'

Felix pushed Asher away so he could see his son's face. 'I'm okay, see. I'm fine now.'

'It all got too much?' Asher said. It was a phrase Felix used a lot when Asher was experiencing *big feelings*, a way to explain how being overwhelmed could make you feel.

'Yeah, it all got too much, but I'm okay now. We'll be fine, I promise.'

Eli walked into the kitchen and placed his phone on the worktop.

'What did she say?' Felix said.

Eli glanced at Asher before speaking. 'She said that she couldn't help. That what she told you was all she knew. She's pissed at you, really pissed.'

'I know,' Felix said.

'You said *pissed,'* Asher said, chancing a smile at Eli.

'Sometimes swear words are the most appropriate words to use,' Eli said, placing a hand on Asher's shoulder. 'What did Lilith say?'

'I left a message,' Felix said.

'Yeah, that sounds about right.'

'Well, you and Asher are staying here until this blows over.'

'Are you sure?' Felix said. There was no point pretending he wasn't relieved by the offer.

'Of course. We just need to come up with a plan.'

'Can you smell that?' Asher said. He leant his head back and sniffed the air.

The scent of burning rubber brushed past Felix.

'What is that?' he said, pushing Asher gently to his feet.

Felix looked to Eli.

'I don't know. I don't...' Eli said.

# Fur Baby Blues

The air turned thick; hot. It filled Eli's throat and sat there, a heavy, cloying weight.

Specs's barking erupted from the living room. The dog threw himself into the kitchen, looking for something. The acrid scent of burning stung Eli's eyes as smoke filled the room.

'Get out of here,' Eli said. He ran to the back door and flung it open, pushing his nephew and brother out first. Specs snapped at his ankles, making sure he followed the others.

They backed away from the house as smoke plumed out of the open door.

'What the-' Felix said. His hand was clamped around Asher's.

*Good,* Eli thought. *He's keeping Asher safe. That's the main thing.*

'Get to the end of the garden,' Eli said. Specs's strained barks snapped at the air. His eyes were fixed on the kitchen door. The fur on his back spiked. He was in attack mode.

'I need to check something,' Eli said. He ran down the narrow alley between his house and his neighbours' and into the front garden. The front of the house was perfect. Nothing was out of place. No smoke. No heat. No burning smell.

'What the fuck?' he whispered under his breath. He approached the house with caution. He seemed to remember having read a news story about somebody who died after opening the front door to their house without realising that there was a small fire inside. When the outside air met the small flame inside, *woosh*, fireball. He touched the door handle with the back of his hand, to check if it was hot. It wasn't. He turned the handle and inched the door open. Nothing. The hallway looked as it always did. It smelled of the plug-in air freshener that sat next to the coat rack.

As Eli approached the kitchen, he stopped again. Smelled the air. Things *seemed* normal. Completely and utterly normal. He repeated what he'd done with the front door, touching the doorknob with the back of his hand to check whether it was hot to the touch. Nope. And so he slowly opened the door. It released a long creak, but nothing else. He peered into the kitchen. Normal. Fucking normal. No smoke. No rubber. No… nothing. Just nothing.

He shook his head, trying to wrap his mind around what was happening. He'd always been the sane one. The stable one. He'd never once questioned his own sanity. But this, *this*, caused him to question everything.

His socked foot hit the tile floor and everything shifted.

Burning rubber. Smoke so thick he couldn't see anything. Heat. Heat so intense it felt like his skin would melt from his bones. His eyes stung and watered. He reached out his hand to feel for the table, creeping forward with closed eyes. If he opened them even a crack, it felt like acid had been poured into them. The heat felt like needles against his skin, like he was being cooked alive. He had to get out. Get to the back door, or retrace his steps. He daren't turn back, scared to lose his sense of direction in the thick smoke.

His shin hit the burning metal of his dining chair. He was on the right track. He just had to keep moving forward. The smoke filled his lungs, sharp pain coursed through his chest. He pulled his t-shirt over his mouth and tried to breathe slowly, steadily, through his nose. Fog swam through his mind, muddying it. What was he doing? He couldn't remember. He couldn't think. He couldn't-

Eli didn't realise he was falling until his head bounced off the tiled floor.

Warm heat pooled under him. He shouldn't open his eyes, but he didn't remember why.

'This is how it felt to die. I felt everything. Now you will too.' Jenna's voice. But Jenna was dead. She died a long time ago. It didn't make sense.

When Specs ran to the kitchen door and into the billowing smoke, Felix had only a split second to make a decision. Follow Specs, or stay with Asher.

'Stay here. Do not move. If I don't come out, go to the neighbour and call the police.'

Asher began to protest but Felix didn't wait. He ran after the dog, throwing his elbow up to shield his face and eyes from the smoke.

'Specs!' Felix yelled.

The dense smoke filled every inch of the kitchen. He couldn't see a thing.

'Specs?' he said, listening intently for any sounds. He could barely open his eyes against the burning smoke.

'Fuck, fuck,' Felix exhaled. He pushed forward, sliding his feet along the floor. He didn't want to step on Specs, or Eli, by mistake.

'Where are you?' Felix said. 'Specs.'

Snuffling. A quiet, pained bark.

'Specs?' Felix said. With one arm across his face, and one out in front, he shuffled in the direction of the noise. His shoe hit something soft.

'Specs?' he said. He knelt down and patted at the floor with his hand.

A body.

'Eli? Eli?' He had no choice but to remove his arm from his face. He used his hands to find purchase. It was definitely a t-shirt that he felt. He moved his hands outwards to find Eli's arms. His fingers brushed against fur.

'Specs?' Felix said.

Felix slipped his hands under Eli's armpits and pulled. Eli was a dead weight. Felix didn't want to think about what that meant.

The caustic smoke seemed to thicken, to solidify. Felix dragged Eli with every ounce of strength he could muster.

'Come on,' he said through gritted teeth. 'Come on.'

The smoke fought with him, pushing him back into the kitchen.

'No. I have to-'

The heat was unbearable. Felix hadn't noticed it until it overcame him, forcing him to fall to his knees.

'This is how it felt to die,' Jenna's voice said in his ear. He could feel the wetness against his skin.

'You're not her,' he said. 'You're not her.'

'The smoke choked me, and then I burned alive. Do you want to know how that feels?'

'No, please, no,' Felix begged.

A moist exhale and then laughter.

'I'm not done with you yet.'

Felix swayed, dizzy, like he'd climbed off a waltzer at the fair. He couldn't stand. He couldn't walk. He held onto one of Eli's arms and yanked, crawling with jolting, unsteady movements. The smoke was thinner on the floor. He could do it. He knew he could. Almost there. But he was tired. So tired.

Sharp pain erupted in his forearm. A bite. A reminder to keep going.

'Specs,' Felix said. His voice was hoarse, burned dry. 'I can do it.'

Felix started again, pulling his brother. He fell out of the door and onto the concrete patio, keeping his grip on Eli, who fell after him.

His eyes cleared. His throat cleared. He was okay.

*Eli.*

Eli was laid partially on top of him, but he was breathing. Felix could hear the breaths. Specs frantically licked Eli's face. Thick red blood blossomed out from the back of Eli's head, turning Felix's t-shirt a murky shade of brown.

'Fuck,' Felix said. He pulled himself out from under Eli and turned him onto his side. His legs rested awkwardly on the single step, one of his feet landing in the kitchen. The kitchen that was no longer full of smoke. Or burning rubber. Or unbearable heat. The kitchen that was, again, just a kitchen.

There was no time to dwell on that. Felix gently ran his fingers through his brother's hair to find the source of the bleeding. A small gash. He must have banged his head pretty hard to knock himself out. That had to be what happened. Felix was no nurse, but he knew that being knocked out meant Eli was in danger of becoming concussed, which could be bad. He'd also need a couple of stitches. But he was alive.

'Dad?' Asher said, standing over him and peering down; eyes wide with terror. 'Is he dead?'

'No. He's just bumped his head pretty badly. He'll be okay. We have to call an ambulance though.'

'No ambulance,' Eli said. 'I'm fine, but Jesus, my head hurts. Paracetamol.'

Hearing Eli speak sent Specs into a fury of tail wags and Staffy cries.

'You're going to A&E. You need to be stitched up.'

'I'm fine.'

'Like hell you are,' Felix said.

Eli tried to roll onto his back so he could sit up.

'Jesus, fuck,' he said, his hand raising to his head.

'Yeah, I bet,' Felix said.

'You're going to the hospital.'

'But what about-' Eli looked back at the kitchen. 'It's gone.'

Felix didn't know what to say, and so he nodded his head.

'I heard her. I heard Jenna.' Eli glanced quickly at Asher and then back at Felix.

'I did too.' Felix turned to Asher. 'It isn't your mum. I promise you that. Whatever it is, it's, it's pretending to be her to hurt us. I need you to remember that, Asher. Promise you'll remember.'

'Yes,' Asher said.

'You stay there for a second,' Felix said to Eli. 'I'm going to get you a drink of water and a tea towel for your head. Stay with him Ash. And then we're going to the hospital.'

Felix inhaled deeply. His throat felt fine, not even so much as a twinge of pain. The smoke, the pain, the smell, all of it had to have been an illusion. It didn't hurt him. Maybe it couldn't hurt him, not physically, at least. Eli got hurt because he fell. Yes, he fell as a result of the illusion, but the illusion itself didn't leave any lasting damage.

*What about Asher?* The thought hit him like a freight train. Whatever it was *had* hurt Asher. It had left marks. So why didn't it hurt Eli or Felix this time?

Felix braced himself as he walked into the kitchen, unsure of what would greet him.

# FOUND YOU

There was no way on earth Eli was leaving Specs alone in the house while he went to A&E. The poor dog was likely more confused than they were. Instead, Eli instructed Felix to take Specs to the neighbour's house. Mrs Birch, a widow in her late sixties, loved nothing more than looking after Specs. When Felix explained what had happened, Mrs Birch attempted to hide her excitement about borrowing Specs for a little while, and feigned concern for Eli. After that, Felix deposited Eli at the hospital with strict instructions to call when he was finished.

'We're not staying?' Asher said as Eli climbed out of the car holding the tea towel to the back of his skull.

'No, we have another job to do.'

Eli nodded. Felix didn't have to explain what he was planning on doing. Finding Lilith was the only logical next step. After what had just happened, they had nowhere else to turn, except back to the source.

'Do not go home alone, call me when you're done,' Felix said, reiterating his instructions one last time.

'I will,' Eli promised. He walked slowly through the automatic doors of their local A&E. Felix wanted to go with him. He *should* have gone with him. But he needed to get to Lilith, and quickly. Eli was safe in the hospital, but what would happen when they returned home was anybody's guess.

'You getting in the front?' Felix said to Asher.

'Yeah,' he said, hopping out of the back of the car and climbing into the passenger seat. 'Where are we going?'

'We're going to find Lilith.'

'Why?' Asher said. 'She's a fraud, you said that.'

'Well, fraud or not, she did something to us, and we need her to fix it.'

'But what if she can't?'

'Then we'll have to figure something else out.'

'What did Nanna say?'

'Nothing very helpful,' Felix said. He kept his eyes on the road, not wanting to see the disappointment in Asher's face.

'How do you know where Lilith is?'

'Her business address is listed as her home address. The power of Google.' Felix attempted to keep his voice light and cheery, for the sake of his son. They both knew it was a veil to mask how he was really feeling, but neither acknowledged it.

'Where does she live?'

'Not far. Just off the M1. It'll only take us an hour.'

'Shouldn't you ring first to check she's there?'

Felix smiled. 'She isn't answering my calls, so she probably doesn't want to see us.'

'Oh, okay,' Asher said. 'Will she be mad at me?'

'Mad at you?' Felix said. 'Why would she be?'

'Because we tricked her and then we told on her. And then everything went wrong.'

'Ash, no, she won't be mad at you. None of this is your fault. It's my fault. I shouldn't have invited her into our lives. I should have just let her continue tricking other people. It wasn't my business. I thought I was doing the right thing, but I dragged you into it. This shouldn't be happening to you.' Felix's knuckles turned a startling white on the steering wheel.

'But she didn't do it on purpose?' Asher said.

Felix paused, gathering his thoughts. 'No, I don't think she did. But that doesn't mean she can't help us.'

Asher nodded. 'Okay. Can we have the radio on?'

'Sure,' Felix said. He clicked on *Planet Rock,* his and Asher's favourite station, and turned up the dial. They drove the rest of the way without speaking.

Lilith lived in a small village that appeared to accommodate more cattle than people. It wasn't at all what Felix had expected. The tiny thatched cottage sat back from a single track road. The only place to park the car was on Lilith's driveway, which felt rude, but he had no choice.

'Stay in the car,' he said to Asher.

Felix balled his fists as he walked up the uneven path. He would not let his emotions get the better of him. He was furious with her, and with himself, but he needed her help. He needed *her.* And if that meant him getting down on his hands and knees and begging, then he would do exactly that.

He pushed the doorbell, listened for the chime ring inside, and waited for what felt like an eternity. Just as he was about to push the bell again, the door flew open, and Lilith peered out at him.

'Nope,' she said, shaking her head. She attempted to pull the door closed but Felix wedged his foot in the gap.

'Please,' Felix said. 'I need to talk to you.'

'You're a psycho,' Lilith bit. Upon closer inspection, Felix noticed she was looking bedraggled. Her face was free from make-up and her hair was scraped back into a greasy bun.

'I wouldn't be here if it wasn't important,' he said. He glanced back at the car and saw Asher's face pushed up against the window. Lilith tilted her head as she followed his action. Her face softened.

'What do you want?' she said.

'You know what I want. Things were fine before you came into our home. Now, fuck, I don't know how to explain it, but we're being attacked, targeted, or something. An entity, a demon, whatever the hell you want to call it. It's ruining our lives. Do you know what happened to me today?'

Lilith didn't respond, but that was okay, Felix didn't expect an answer.

'My brother's house turned into a literal oven. It was so hot. It filled with smoke. You couldn't see your hand in front of your face. And the smell, *the smell*: burning rubber. My brother's house turned into what my wife felt when she died. The entity, or whatever the fuck it is, is pretending to be her. It uses her voice. It told me that that was how she felt when she died. That she felt everything. Can you even imagine?'

'I didn't do anything to you. I don't know what's happening to you. What I do, it isn't real. Haven't you realised that by now? It's not real. I'm a fake. You knew that. I don't believe in any of it. None of it is real. You're fucking with me. You have to be fucking with me to get me to stop. Fine, I stop. I give up. I won't do it anymore. I won't-'

'You think I'm messing with you? I told you that I can see spirits; only my family knows that. I told you why I hired you. Whatever is in my house, it isn't a spirit. I need your help. You brought something in with you and now it's ruining my life.'

'You tricked me into coming to your house. You admitted that. You wanted people to know that I'm a fraud. I can't take it anymore. Please just stop. I'll quit. I won't ever do it again. That video…'

'I'm telling the truth,' Felix said. 'I need your help.'

'You can't be. This stuff isn't real. None of it is. It's the power of suggestion. I tell people their ghosts are gone and so they're gone. I tell them that their dead child has passed over and that they're safe and happy. That's what they want to hear, and so I tell them. What's so bad about that? Why are you doing this to me?'

'Doing this to you?' Felix echoed. 'Why am I doing this to you?' Felix took a deep breath and checked himself. He wasn't there to argue with her. There was no point in that. 'I need your help.'

'There's nothing I can do to help you. Whatever is happening to you, if it's even real-'

'-is your fault,' Felix said, finishing her sentence.

She shook her head slowly. 'I don't know what to do. I don't believe in this stuff, but that video, it looked so real.'

'It *was* real,' Felix said. 'And you're my best shot at getting rid of whatever the fuck it is.'

Lilith placed her hands on her hips and bit down hard on her lip.

'Fine, okay, but I have no idea what to do,' she said.

'Thank you,' Felix said. He almost collapsed to the floor in relief.

'Let me grab my bag,' she said. She turned back into her house. Felix stuck a thumb up to Asher, whose nose was still pressed against the glass.

Felix recognised the bag that Lilith heaved along with her. It was the bag of tricks she'd brought for her 'cleansing service'. As much as Felix knew the items in that bag would have little effect on the malevolent being currently tormenting them, it felt somewhat comforting to know that she was taking this seriously.

Felix moved his foot out of the way of the door so Lilith could lock it behind her. She walked to the car painfully slowly, like a hanged man on his way to the noose.

# An Archangel

'We're not going to your house?' Lilith said as they pulled up outside Eli's home.

'No. This is my brother's house.'

She nodded. 'Because it follows you.' She blinked rapidly, like she couldn't believe she'd not made the connection.

'Ash, do you want to go and get Specs? Doesn't look like Uncle Eli is home yet.'

Asher jumped out of the car and walked to Mrs Birch's house. He knocked at the door and waited for it to open.

'Come on then,' Felix said to Lilith, ushering her towards the house.

Once inside, Lilith dumped her bag in the hallway and looked around. The house looked perfectly normal. He could see that she was expecting something far more sinister.

'It seems to always revert to normal after,' Felix said.

'Hmm,' Lilith said.

'What?' he asked.

'Nothing.'

'Tell me,' Felix said, more forcefully than he'd intended.

'You said your brother was a graphic designer?'

'Yes.' Felix attempted to follow her train of thought but had no idea where she was going with it.

'He could have faked the videos.'

'Why would he do that?' Lilith was grasping at straws, trying to reason with what she had seen. It made sense. There was a disconnect between what your brain knew to be impossible, and what those videos showed. He wouldn't have believed it either.

'To get me here? You obviously have some kind of vendetta against me.'

Felix laughed. The door opened and Specs barrelled in toward Lilith. He jumped at her, tail wagging, and almost knocked her to the floor.

'Hi puppy,' Lilith said, scratching him behind the ears as he leaned his front paws against her stomach.

Felix took that as a good sign. The Specs seal of approval. Maybe she wasn't entirely evil.

'Let's not waste any time,' Felix said, hoping that Lilith didn't truly believe that he would coerce her here for some nefarious reason.

Lilith smiled down at Specs and gently pushed him off her. The dog had worked his magic.

'I have no idea if this is going to work, but these solutions, these *spells*, I suppose, have been passed down from generation to generation. All old wives' tales are based on truths. Maybe we should wait for your brother to get back.'

'Why?' Asher said. He shut the door behind him and went to stand beside Felix.

'Because I'm going to be doing protection spells, and he should be here for that if he's involved.'

'Well, he's currently waiting to be stitched up at A&E, so we could be waiting a while…'

'Okay. We'll do his when he gets back. Come here.' She beckoned to Asher and Felix and reached out her hands. 'Hold my hands, and then hold each other's.'

They did as they were asked. Lilith's hands were cold as ice.

'Now, I want you to picture a pure white light around you, and around his house. Close your eyes.'

Felix would have scoffed if he could think of any other alternative. His Google searches for ridding yourself of demons and evil spirits had shown up nothing useful.

'Now, picture the light glowing brighter and brighter.'

Felix tried, really tried. He could tell by the way Asher was gripping his hand tightly that he was trying too.

'Now, I'm going to say a prayer,' Lilith said.

'But we're not religious,' Felix said, aware of what his mother had said about how only those who truly believe in a religion can benefit from its protection.

'Then think of it as a spell. Think of St. Michael as a being of protection, not an archangel.'

'Okay,' Felix said. He kept his eyelids closed tightly and listened to Lilith's words, trying to *feel* each one.

'St. Michael the Archangel, defend us in battle, be our protection against the wickedness and snares of the devil. May God rebuke him we humbly pray; and do thou, O Prince of the Heavenly host, by the power of God, cast into hell Satan and all the evil spirits who prowl about the world seeking the ruin of souls. Amen.'

*Seeking to ruin souls,* didn't make Felix feel entirely comfortable. It seemed to describe what they were experiencing with far too much accuracy for his liking.

'Did it work?' Asher asked.

Felix opened his eyes to find Asher peeking at Lilith.

'I suppose we won't know just yet,' Lilith said.

The answer didn't satisfy Asher, his face twisted with worry.

'Right, onto the sage.'

'Sage? Like last time?' Felix said.

'Yes, sage like last time. I'm going through every trick I know. Maybe one of them will work. Better safe than sorry.'

Felix couldn't argue with that.

From within her bag, Lilith pulled out a smudge stick of sage. The boulder in the pit of Felix's stomach alerted him to the fact that this was happening almost exactly like the last time Lilith was in their home.

As she promised, Lilith did exactly what she had last time, if a little more thoroughly. Eli's house smelled like incense, and lavender, and sage, and God only knew what else. When she'd finished, Lilith simply said, 'Right, that's it.'

'That's it?' Felix said.

'Yes. I told you. I don't know what is happening to you, or why, but this is all I know to do. I've done everything I can. Now, I'd like to go home please, can you take me home?'

Specs nudged Lilith's leg with his nose and looked up at her. She bent down and ruffled the fur on his head.

'What if it didn't work?'

Lilith shrugged, an action that made him irrationally angry.

'I need you to stay to see if it worked,' Felix said.

Lilith shook her head.

'Please,' Asher's voice came from behind him. 'Please stay to check it worked.'

Lilith looked like she was about to argue but the words fell silent in her mouth. 'Fine. I'll stay a while longer.'

'I'll take you home in the morning,' Felix said. 'We should know if it's worked by then, surely.'

'Fine, okay,' Lilith said.

Felix had expected her to put up a fight. He eyed her warily. Guilt. That was the only explanation for her change in demeanour. Asher had managed to get under her skin. He was good at that. People were always drawn to him.

Asher walked over to Lilith and wrapped his arms around her. He didn't hug strangers. Ever.

'Thank you,' Felix said.

'You can take the sofa, if that's okay. I'll get you some fresh sheets.'

'Okay,' she replied. The word was clipped.

The door creaked open, 'Hello?' Eli's voice sounded from the hallway.

'In here,' Felix said.

Eli walked into the kitchen, a bandage around his head.

'Why didn't you call me?' Felix said.

'I got a taxi, figured it was easier.'

'Are you okay? Did you need many stitches?' Felix asked.

'Yeah, a good few, I didn't ask how many.' He turned his attention to Lilith. 'You must be Lilith.'

She nodded and reached out her hand, Eli took it politely.

'Thank you for coming,' Eli said. 'So, what did I miss?'

Lilith quickly recounted what she'd done in order to ward off evil from the house.

'And she's staying the night,' Felix added.

'And you think that will do it?' Eli said. His question was genuine, there was no malice in his words.

'I have no idea,' Lilith said. 'As I said, I'm a fake, I know nothing about actual hauntings or whatever this is. I'm not sure I even believe in the supernatural.'

'Oh, it's real,' Eli said. 'But, do you know what? I hope you leave tomorrow still not believing, I really do. Hopefully, whatever you've done will fix this shit because this family has been through enough, you know?'

Lilith nodded silently.

'So, what do we do now? Do we sit and wait for something to happen? Do we carry on as normal?' Felix said, looking between Lilith and Eli.

'It's impossible to prove a negative, that's the thing, right? We can't prove that what Lilith has done will work, until it doesn't, so…'

'We could watch a film?' Asher said, his voice cutting through the tension. 'Maybe order food, I'm hungry and Uncle Eli never has any food in.'

'Do you know what, that sounds like a plan,' Felix said. In the whirlwind of the day, he had completely forgotten that Asher hadn't had lunch. It was getting late, well past dinner time. He could add that to the number of ways he'd failed as a parent, he supposed.

'Pizza?' Eli said.

'Sounds good to me,' Felix said, as Asher nodded in assent.

'What about you, Lilith? Pizza sound good?'

'Is it gluten free?' she said.

'I don't think so,' Eli said. Felix caught his eye and held back a laugh. Lilith was really living up to the stereotypes.

Eli ordered the food, a vegan pizza for Lilith, which was the best they could manage, and they crowded into the living area. Specs jumped onto the sofa and filled half of it. Nobody had the heart to move him. Asher curled up around Specs, and Lilith slotted into the gap at the end of the sofa.

'And now we wait,' Eli said. Felix appreciated that he was trying to lighten the mood, but it was a swing and a miss. Felix sat with his back against the sofa, while Eli lounged in the armchair.

Asher chose *A Bugs Life,* one of his favourite films from when he was younger. A comfort film, Felix noted.

The doorbell sounded and Specs jumped to life, barking in the general direction of the door, but not bothering to leave the sofa.

'I'll get it,' Felix said. As he walked to the door, a familiar scent bit at his senses. Burning. A charred, dirty smell, like burned meat. He decided that it had to be the pizzas they'd ordered. It made logical sense. Although, something niggled at him. The smell was so similar to what he'd experienced in the kitchen earlier.

Felix opened the door and took the pizza boxes from the teenager.

'Thank you,' he said, shutting the door.

The smell was more intense than before.

'What the hell?' he muttered to himself, opening the top pizza box.

Disgust crawled over his skin. Bile threatened to climb his throat.

'No, no,' Felix repeated the words, over and over like a prayer.

'What is it?' Eli said. He noted Felix's expression, his own eyes widening in question.

'It looks like burnt skin. Tell me that's not skin.'

Eli peered into the pizza box.

'Oh god, I think I'm going to be sick.'

# On Our Own

'What the fuck is that?' Lilith said. She stared down at the dropped pizza, lying splayed like an open corpse on the floor.

The words barely washed over Eli as he retched into the downstairs toilet. The toilet, situated under the stairs, meant that Eli was still in the thick of it. He could hear Felix trying to herd Asher back into the living area. There was no way Asher should see that.

'It smells so bad,' Asher said.

'You need to stay in there. Look after Specs for me, he'll be scared.'

More bile poured out of Eli's stomach, burning his throat, and splashing into the toilet. His head pounded fiercely.

'Put it outside for god's sake,' Eli said between bursts of foul-tasting vomit.

He wasn't sure who did as he asked, but the door was opened and, a moment later, it was closed again.

'It was burned skin,' Felix said.

'Animal skin. Who would do that? Protestors?' Lilith said.

'It didn't look like animal skin,' Felix said, causing Eli to retch again.

'How would you know?' Lilith asked.

'It smelled exactly the same as the house did earlier,' Felix said. 'When Eli got hurt.'

'Oh,' Lilith said.

'I don't think what you did worked,' Eli called from the toilet.

'Shit,' Lilith said.

Felix could hear the genuine frustration in her voice. He found it strangely comforting.

'So, what's our next steps?' Felix said.

Eli rinsed out his mouth with cold water from the tap and rejoined them. The rhythmic pounding in his temple further amplified.

'I don't know. I don't know. What are our options?' Eli said.

'Is there somebody we can reach out to? An expert on this kind of thing?' Felix asked.

Both Eli and Felix turned to look at Lilith.

'I have no idea,' she said, her voice raising to a higher pitch. 'I'm not… I don't… Fuck.'

She shook her head in irritation.

Eli wanted to scream at her. He was usually calm, painfully so, all his exes said, but he was about to lose it with her.

'You *should* know what to do. You don't go messing around in things like this without knowing what you're doing, surely?' Eli snapped.

'I didn't believe it was real. I didn't. I just-'

'You were trying to make a quick buck.' Eli finished her sentence.

Eli noticed Felix had his mobile in his hand. 'Who are you calling?' he asked.

'Mum, again. She knew something, more than she was telling me. I know it.'

'But why didn't she tell you before?'

'I don't know.' Felix shook his head in desperation.

Lilith also had her phone in her hand, she was tapping away at the screen vigorously. 'What are you doing?' Eli asked.

'I attend conferences on this kind of thing sometimes, you know, to connect with others. I have some contacts. I mean, I always thought they were making shit up like me but maybe they weren't. If there's a chance-'

'And you didn't tell us this before?' Eli said.

'I didn't believe you before!' she yelled.

'Mum's not answering her phone. It is getting on a bit, maybe she's in bed,' Felix said.

'Maybe she's busy with her boyfriend,' Eli said.

'Should one of us go and see her?' Felix asked.

'Yeah, I think we should.'

Felix shrunk to a crouch, perching at the bottom of the staircase, putting his head in his hands.

'I did this. This is my fault,' he said.

Eli leaned against the wall. He scraped his hands through his hair. He wasn't going to disagree with Felix, he *had* brought it on himself. And he should feel bad about it.

'Any luck?' he said to Lilith.

'I'm messaging every person I know. Every person that could possibly be real.'

'And?'

'None of them are answering!'

There was a desperation in her tone that he was pleased to hear. She was taking this seriously now.

'I'm going to leave Mum a message,' Felix said. I'll give it an hour and then I'll go through and see her again. If she knows something, why won't she tell us? I don't get it.'

'What's this about your mum?' Lilith said, without looking up from her phone screen.

'She's like Felix,' Eli answered. 'She sees spirits, people who haven't passed on. But she's very, I don't know how to describe it, she's very in touch with all that paranormal, supernatural stuff. She knows a lot about that kind of stuff. Felix went to see her yesterday and told her everything that had been happening. Of course, this was before my *accident*. But she was very cryptic in her response. She said we had two options, do an exorcism, which would only work if we all *believe* in that kind of thing, which we don't, we're atheists, although, after this, who knows?'

'And the second option?' Lilith prompted.

'Kill the entity when it possesses somebody,' Eli said.

'The entity?' Lilith said.

'That's what she said. She called it an entity.'

Lilith continued tapping on her screen. She began to read aloud, 'Supernatural creatures, forces, and events are believed by some people to exist or happen, although they are impossible according to scientific laws. That's the definition of an entity. It's an umbrella term for lots of different things. So that's not particularly helpful. We don't even know what *it* is. What's doing this? Is it an energy? Is it a force? Is it a ghost? A spirit, a poltergeist, a demon? We don't even know what we're fighting against.'

'Shit, you're right. You're absolutely right. I hate this,' Eli said. 'How can you fight against something when you don't know what it is?'

'I've left a message for Mum,' Felix said. 'Any responses Lilith?'

'Not yet,' she said. 'I've copied and pasted the same message to everybody I know who may have an idea of what to do.'

Eli suspected that there was a reason they weren't answering Lilith. If they had any semblance of decency, they would find what she did to others abhorrent.

'I can't just sit here. I need to be doing something. What can I do?' Felix said.

'Research. You're about on the same level of understanding as I am, so research. You won't find many, if any, peer reviewed papers on hauntings, or whatever this is, but maybe there will be some other things we can try. We're desperate,' Lilith said.

'You okay in there Ash?' Eli shouted into the living room. Asher had been too quiet.

'I'm researching. I was already doing that before you asked,' he called back.

A smile tugged at Eli's lips. He was such a good kid.

'What have you searched for?' Eli asked, poking his head into the living room. Asher was staring intently at his tablet.

'How to get rid of a demon,' he said. He couldn't argue with Asher's method.

'Did you find anything?'

'Yes. It says to rule out non-demonic causes first. We've done that. Second, it said to burn sage, Lilith did that. And the last one was to say a prayer. We did that too. I think we're fucked.'

Eli barked out a laugh at Asher's language. Now wasn't the time to correct his use of profanity. Plus, it was accurate. They were fucked.

'Everything I find is linked to mental illness,' Felix said. 'People are blaming mental illness for causing all kinds of paranormal-like experiences. I can't imagine we're all suffering from the same delusion, can you?'

'Faith in Jesus is required to get rid of demons,' Lilith said, peering up from her phone. 'Not sure that will work for us.'

'Did somebody message you back?' Eli said.

'No, I Googled it. Wait,' she said. 'Emmanuel answered.'

'Emmanuel?' Felix asked, still crouched on the floor, hovering over his phone.

'Emmanuel Stark, he's a parapsychologist. One of the world's leading ones, according to him. I'm not sure there's much competition for that title, to be fair,' Lilith said. Eli wanted to comment about the hypocrisy of her statement, but he kept that to himself. Lilith was helping them, for now, so there was no point starting an argument.

'And what does he say?' Eli said.

'Oh,' Lilith said. Her face fell.

'What?' Eli pushed.

'He said, good luck, and asked if I could film everything we do for evidence.'

'Evidence for what?' Eli asked.

'His research, he's studying demonic possession. He said it's only a matter of time before one of us is possessed by the demon here.'

'Nothing else?' Felix asked. He stood up from his perch.

'Nothing else.'

'Is that even ethical? That he knows what is happening to us and won't help us? Call him. Call him now,' Eli demanded.

Without hesitation, Lilith called Emmanuel. Eli watched closely to make sure she was doing as he'd asked. It rang and rang and rang.

'He's ignoring you. He's online,' Eli said.

'He's just messaged back,' Lilith said.

'He said that there has been no concrete evidence of demonic possession, and therefore there has been no concrete evidence of what to do in order to combat one. The Church argues that exorcism works, but that's a fairly contentious subject. He also said that killing the vessel, which is what your mum suggested, likely won't work either because the entity will move to somebody else. That being said, he did ask, again, that we film what we do.'

'Fuck him,' Felix said. 'What kind of parapsychologist doesn't know how to get rid of a demon?'

'Most people who study parapsychology do it from the perspective that they believe there's a logical, non-paranormal, reason for everything that happens. They're essentially historians focusing on folklore.'

'So we're on our own?' Eli said, walking into the living room to check on Asher and Specs.

'Yes, we're on our own,' Lilith said. 'We're on our own.'

# Flying High

Goosebumps flecked Felix's skin. The house was freezing. *Had it always been freezing?* He wasn't sure.

'Woah,' Lilith said, answering his question, visibly trembling.

Warm breath shushed against his ear. He turned, expecting to see Eli behind him, but Eli wasn't there.

'Kitty?' A single long exhale.

His blood ran cold in his veins.

'Kitty? This is your fault. Why would you do this to our son? Don't you love him?'

'Did you hear that?' Felix said.

Nobody answered him.

'Lilith? Did you hear that?'

Lilith's eyes were wide. Her jaw tensed. Her head was cocked like she was straining to hear something.

'Lilith?'

'I didn't. It isn't my fault.' Her words were barely audible.

'Lilith?' Felix approached her, placing his hands on her shoulders.

'It was an accident. I'm sorry,' she moaned. She looked over her shoulder, not acknowledging Felix's presence. She appeared to be listening to somebody Felix couldn't see.

'Lilith!' he said, louder. He squeezed her shoulders, trying to bring her back to the present.

'No, no, no!'

Her eyes snapped to his. They widened more than he thought was physically possible.

Complete terror masked her face. Her arms came up to his face, throwing his hands from her shoulders. Her sharp fingernails met his cheeks, slicing down in ragged clumps.

'What are you doing?' Felix shouted, stepping back.

'Leave me alone. I didn't do it!'

Lilith's fist lashed out at Felix, catching him off guard. A blinding pain flashed through his temple.

'Stop it!' he snarled, pushing her back.

'No, leave me alone. Don't hurt me! I didn't mean to!' Her voice shook with each word.

'Lilith, it's Felix. I won't hurt you. I haven't hurt you.' He attempted to contort his voice into a calming tone, the kind he used on Asher when he was upset. It didn't work, Lilith lunged again.

'Stop it!' Felix yelled.

'Felix!' Eli said.

Specs's barking sounded like an alarm, calling Felix into the living room.

'Asher, no,' Eli said. 'FELIX!' The desperation in Eli's voice tore through Felix.

He ran to the living room and stopped on the threshold, unable to comprehend the sight before him.

Asher floated above Eli's head. *Floated.* His body was horizontal, but limp. His limbs hung down towards the floor, like a child picking up a ragdoll. Eli grabbed at Asher's wrists, trying to pull him back down.

'Felix! Help me, he won't…'

Felix finally convinced his limbs to move. He felt like he was walking through soup, like time had slowed. He looked down and noted Specs jumping, snarling, trying to grab hold of Asher's shirt or trousers. Specs's old body couldn't jump high enough. The dog whined with effort, and kept trying.

Reaching out with a shaking hand, Felix touched Asher's hand. He almost pulled it away. His skin felt like fire.

'Asher?' Felix said, his voice wavered. He wanted to ask what Asher was doing, why he was floating above their heads. He couldn't quite grasp what was happening in front of him. That *something,* this demon, this entity, whatever the fuck it was, was *touching* his son. It was doing something to him. Through the fog of racing thoughts, Felix looked at Asher's face, trying to determine if his son was in any pain.

'Oh God,' he said, shrinking to his knees.

Asher's head hung backward, his mouth was contorted, his chin jutting to the side, hanging open. Red oozed from within, dribbling out of his mouth, and into his hair. Drip, drip, dripping onto the floor. He couldn't consider what the red stuff was. He couldn't because that would mean that Asher was… No, he wouldn't finish the thought.

Red began to pool on the floor. Felix was vaguely aware of Specs, and of Eli attempting to rag his son out of the air. He stared at the floor, watching the puddle grow.

'Kitty, you did this to him. This is your fault.'

'No, no I didn't,' Felix snarled back at the thing that definitely wasn't Jenna. He knew better than to look for the source of the voice. Nothing would be there.

'Your one job was to keep him safe. That's all. You just had to get involved with the fraudulent psychic. You just couldn't leave it alone. You had to prove that you were better than her. Textbook narcissist. I should never have married you. I should never have given you a son.' A pause; the room bursting with silence. 'LOOK AT WHAT YOU'VE DONE TO HIM.'

Wicked laughter broke out from behind him. Felix wouldn't look. He wouldn't give *it* the satisfaction. The voice changed, mimicking the way you'd speak to a toddler. 'He's dying Felix, and it's all your fault. I'm going to slit his throat and eat him raw.'

'No!' Felix cried. He stood on unsteady legs and reached out again to his son. His eyes met Eli's. Eli who had never given up trying to save Asher. Eli who hadn't collapsed to the floor in weakness. He met Eli's eyes, saw the trails of tears lining his cheeks. There was a ferocity in them that Felix had never witnessed in his brother before. A lion protecting his cub.

Felix nodded slightly, barely imperceptible; telling his brother that he was back.

For a terrible moment, Eli thought that his brother's mind had snapped. He thought that he'd lost Felix. But he was back. Felix balled his fists into Asher's shirt and began to pull with all his might, the muscles and tendons straining in his neck.

'Come on,' Felix snarled.

Eli tried to find purchase on Asher's body, which hovered two feet above their heads, almost at the ceiling. He pulled on Asher's arm, throwing all of his body weight into it and praying that it would be enough. But Asher was frozen solid. No matter what they did, he didn't move.

The floor was slick with blood. *How much blood can a human body hold?* Eli thought, and then forced the words away into the recesses of his mind. There was no way that the world could exist without Asher in it. Asher would be fine. He had to be fine.

Eli locked both of his hands around one of Asher's wrists.

'Get the other,' Eli ordered Felix.

Felix moved instantly, doing as asked.

'On three,' Eli said. 'One, two, three.'

Together, they put their entire body weights behind pulling Asher to the floor.

*CRACK.*

The noise sent shock waves through Eli. Asher's shoulders hung at different angles than they had before. It looked like his shoulder blades had slid further around his back.

Bile flung itself up Eli's throat. They both staggered back as though they'd been shot.

'Oh my God, oh my God, oh my God.' Felix said the words like a prayer, over and over.

Blood began to bloom like flowers in the back, or underside, Eli supposed, of Asher's clothes.

'Where's that blood coming from?' he said, looking to Felix for an answer. Felix stared up at his son, eyes wide and unbelieving.

Eli pulled back Asher's t-shirt and blood gushed from within it with enough force to knock him off his feet. The pain in his head was returning with a vengeance, but he couldn't think about that, not when Asher was…

Asher's body began to vibrate. A scream erupted from his mouth, swallowing Specs's panicked cries. Asher's head snapped back. The back of his head touched his displaced shoulders. The scream was impossibly long; impossibly loud.

Searching for a new plan, grasping at straws, Eli looked around the room and saw Lilith in the doorway holding up her phone and pointing it toward them. He wasn't sure when the screaming stopped, but at some point it had.

'What the fuck are you doing?' Eli yelled, rushing toward her to snatch the phone.

'He told me to record it. I told you that,' Lilith said.

'And you decided that was a good idea? Fucking hell Lilith, this is our family, not something to be studied. What? Do you think this is going to get you taken seriously? *Lilith Lavelle witnessed a real haunting, a real possession, she deserves our respect.* You said it yourself, they all think you're a fraud.'

Eli snatched the phone from her hand and threw it across the room. It bounced off the wall and landed behind the sofa.

'How many cases of genuine paranormal activity have you seen?' Lilith said, her words rushed, panicked. 'This is it? This is the real deal, and you don't want to record it? This could change the course of history. If you can definitively prove it's real, just think of the consequences!' Lilith stood her ground with her hands placed on her hips. Although she looked scared, frantic even, she didn't back down when Eli stepped closer to her.

'You listen to me,' Eli said. He leaned so close that his nose was almost touching hers. 'My family will not be the one to prove that this is real. My family will not be the sacrifice.'

Lilith shook her head, gritting her teeth. She fixed her eyes on Eli's, challenging him to continue.

'Eli, something's happening.' Felix's voice sliced through the stand-off.

Eli turned on his heel and stared back up at the twisted sight.

Specs's barking faded into oblivion, Eli no longer hearing it.

Asher's body had begun to writhe slowly. Eli watched in horror as his arms bent backward at the elbow until S*NAP*. Eli retched at the noise, at the broken arms; forearms hanging loose to the floor. Asher's eyes were wide, filled with pain, but he didn't make a sound. Eli hoped above all else that Asher couldn't feel what was happening to him. Asher's wrists were next. It looked like somebody was taking their time, forcing his hands backwards until there was no more give. The fingers snapped back one by one. Each bone broke with a sickening snap. The expression on Asher's face didn't change. It was slick with blood. He didn't blink as the blood ran through his eyes, Eli held onto hope that this meant Asher wasn't present in his body for this.

Felix sobbed, his entire body shook vigorously back and forth.

Blood continued to leak from Asher's body as the bones in his legs broke.

'Where is the blood coming from?' Felix asked between sobs.

'It looks like it's coming out of his skin, like sweat?' Lilith whispered from behind where Eli was standing.

'Asher, Asher,' Felix said. 'If you can hear me, I'm here. I'm here. We'll figure this out. We will.'

'What the fuck do you want?' Lilith said. It was clear she'd meant her voice to sound commanding. 'What do you want from us?' She looked at Felix, and then at Eli. 'I didn't believe they were real. I didn't. I didn't believe in any of it. But, whatever *this* is, it wants something from you. Can't you feel it? It needs something. Why else would it do this to an innocent boy?'

'It's doing this because you brought it into our lives,' Felix said, running at Lilith, fist drawn.

'No, it's more than that. I can feel it, can't you?' Lilith said, hands raised to fend off the blow.

'Daddy.'

All three heads looked up at Asher. His neck was still wrenched back in a position that could not have been natural. He looked down at them. Blood dripped from his clothes. His face split into a wide smile, blood coating his teeth, 'Don't worry, Kitty. It's not over just yet. I want to savour this feeling.'

Asher's body dropped like a stone and landed in a crumpled pile on the floor. Felix and Eli dropped to their knees, their hands exploring his body, checking for damage. Eli's eyes met Felix, understanding etched on both of their faces. He was whole. No breaks. No cuts or bruises. Before their eyes, the blood seeped back into his body.

'This is your fault, Daddy. Mummy said it was all your fault.'

'Mummy said that?' Felix said. His hands were clasped tightly on either side of Asher's face.

'Yeah. She's always telling me that. She said that you're trying to kill me, and if you loved me, you wouldn't have told Lilith to come and bring a demon with her. She says she's going to take me with her, but I don't want to go. I don't want to die. I want to stay with you.' Asher stopped speaking and pulled in a deep breath. 'She's going to make you watch her kill me.'

Asher's cheeks were flushed a deep red. Eli couldn't help but think about the blood that had, only moments ago, pooled on the floor, after leaking out of Asher.

'Hey, Asher, no. Your mum isn't here. And, if she was, she wouldn't say things like that. She loved us both. She knew how much I love you. She would never hurt you, and neither would I.'

Asher shook his head vigorously.

'No, she said that you failed us. You failed her, and now she won't stop crying.'

'You can hear her now?' Lilith's voice cut through the room.

Asher's head snapped toward her.

'You can't hear her?' His eyes grew wide and searching. Asher looked from person to person, looking for confirmation that somebody could hear his dead mother crying.

'I can't hear her, Ash,' Eli said.

'I don't think any of us can,' Lilith said, standing tall just behind them.

'Wait,' Asher said. His face paling. 'She's not crying. She's laughing. Why is she laughing?'

'It isn't your mum, Ash,' Eli said. 'You have to know that. Whatever this thing is, it isn't your mum.'

Felix pulled Asher against him, hugging him tightly.

Feeling a wet nose against his cheek, Eli wrapped an arm around Specs. The poor dog was panting hard. 'It's okay Specs. It's okay.' He stroked the soft smooth fur on Specs's back. He could feel the dog shaking under his hand. 'Shhh, it's okay,' he said into Specs's neck.

Until that moment, Eli had always rolled his eyes when he'd heard the phrase *silence is deafening,* but it was. After the screaming, the barking, the snapping bones, the room was filled with silence.

'I'm sorry,' Lilith said.

'You're what?' Eli said, blind fury overcoming him.

'I'm sorry. I didn't mean to. I didn't know it would. It shouldn't have been like this. I didn't believe it was real. I didn't. I promise.'

The apology meant nothing to him. Nothing at all. It took everything in him not to snap.

'Has it stopped? Do you think it's over for now?' Felix asked. The question was redundant; completely pointless. They all knew that this entity, this demon, was unpredictable.

Lilith walked slowly around the room, giving them a wide berth. She picked her phone up off the floor from behind the sofa. The ceiling light reflected on the scratched screen.

'I have another response from Emmanuel Stark,' she said, graciously not mentioning the broken screen. 'He has questions.'

'I thought he'd given up on us,' Eli said.

'So did I. Apparently not. He said he's been thinking more about it and if this is an actual demonic possession, we're fucked. He actually used that word, by the way. But there are some things we can try. He basically said we can throw shit at the wall and see what sticks. But before that, he said that there have been cases of *demonic possession* that were caused by various mental and physical illnesses, and he's presuming we've ruled all that out.' She rolled her eyes, and began to tap furiously on the screen. 'Of course we have, we're not stupid. What an arsehole.'

The phone pinged. 'Okay, he says, we can try to kill the vessel and hope that works, you already said that though, and we can pray that it doesn't go straight into somebody else. If it does, we'd be playing demonic whack-a-mole. Alternatively, we could find what the demon wants and give it to them.'

'And how are we supposed to do that?' Felix said. 'Just ask it? It's pretending to be my dead fucking wife.'

A sob escaped from Asher at those words. 'Shhh.' Felix soothed Asher. 'I'm sorry.'

'I don't know. He says that all demons want something, otherwise why bother possessing a human?'

'What could it possibly want?'

'I was getting to that,' Lilith said. 'Emmanuel says that usually demons want one of three things. First, they may want to cause pain and anguish because they feed off it. Second, they may be looking for a body to control, to live in like a parasite. Or, third, they may want to kill. He says something about how, in some research, and he specifies that none of this is peer reviewed, that demons see human beings as pawns to be toyed with. They may gain energy, power, from causing pain, but the ultimate source of power, is death.' Lilith squinted at the phone, reading ahead. 'And then he asked again if I'd managed to film any of it.'

'Do not send that video to him,' Felix said. 'I don't want my son plastered all over the internet.'

'I wouldn't,' Lilith said. 'You asked me not to. But I told him what had just happened.'

'Good,' Eli said. He watched his brother tense his jaw before turning his attention back to Asher.

'So, did he say anything else? Could you call him? If he's the leading parapsycho-whatever, maybe he has some ideas now other than *best of luck?'*

Lilith lifted her face from the phone and shouted at the air.

'I command you to tell me your name.'

# Lilith's Interlude – 3 Months Ago

The family lived in the middle of the Yorkshire Dales. A beautiful village, well-to-do. The kind of place where the homes had been in families for generations. The email Mrs Sawyer had sent caught Lilith off guard. Her son was very ill, and would be dead in a few weeks, and he'd started talking to something that wasn't there. This *ghost*, as Mrs Sawyer called it, was telling young Albert things from the past, things that the boy could not possibly know if the ghost wasn't real.

It wasn't a new story. Lilith heard of this kind of thing all the time. The unusual information, often unflattering for the family, would usually come from playground gossip, somebody's parents talking about somebody's parents within earshot of the child, and it would get back to the source. That, or the child would find photo albums, or a grandparent would drunkenly spill the family's secrets at Christmas. There was always a valid explanation for *paranormal phenomena*. Always.

Lilith was greeted at the door by Mrs Sawyer, an ageing *soccer mom* who she assumed drove the Chelsea Tractor in the driveway.

'Come in, come in,' she said, opening the door wide.

The house smelled of sickness.

'Albert is upstairs,' she said. Her voice shook and she wrung her hands together.

'Why don't we sit and have a coffee first? Let's have a chat about what's been happening,' Lilith said gently.

'Okay, yeah, that might be best.'

Lilith was led into a cavernous kitchen. Bifold doors lined the garden side of the room. An Aga stood proudly in what seemed to be the trappings of an original fireplace.

'You have a beautiful home,' Lilith said, taking a seat at a dining table that could comfortably fit twelve.

'Thank you. It was built in the 1700s, and was originally the village schoolhouse.'

'So much history,' Lilith said, wondering if it would be impolite to ask Mrs Sawyer to open a window. 'Is Mr Sawyer at work?' she said, instead.

'No, he, well, he died three years ago.' Tears leaked down the perfectly powdered cheeks of Mrs Sawyer.

'I'm sorry to hear that,' Lilith said, leading the conversation towards an explanation.

'It was suicide.' Mrs Sawyer lowered her voice. 'You'd probably find that out from Albert anyway, so why not tell you?' She smiled. It didn't reach her eyes. 'He got arrested for fraud and killed himself before the trial.'

Lilith shook her head. 'I'm sorry that happened.'

'Yeah, me too,' Mrs Sawyer said.

'Has anything changed since we last spoke?' Lilith asked once the silence became too much.

'Yes, it seems that there are two ghosts now. There used to be just one, I think, but he never called it by a name. One of them,' Mrs Sawyer sniffled, 'he calls *Dad,* and the other he calls *Nicolas.'*

Seeing dead relatives was fairly standard as far as Lilith was concerned. Usually, people saw *ghosts* of loved ones, friends or family who had passed away. She assumed Nicolas would fall into one of those categories.

'Who is Nicolas?' Lilith asked.

'I don't know. We don't know a Nicolas.'

*Maybe an imaginary friend,* Lilith thought.

Lilith explained to Mrs Sawyer her usual techniques: the sage, lavender, the cleaning, all the stuff she always did when summoned to cleanse a house. 'I'll leave Albert's room until last.'

Mrs Sawyer nodded and left Lilith to it. She went through her routine as though it was a dance, adding some flair for Mrs Sawyer's benefit. The poor woman looked like she needed it. Mrs Sawyer stayed out of her way, smiling sadly at her whenever Lilith happened to walk by.

'I would like to do Albert's room now, Mrs Sawyer. Could you come with me?'

Mrs Sawyer wiped her already clean hands on her trousers and nodded. Lilith made it a general rule not to be alone with children when she worked, especially sick ones. They reacted very strangely to their parents bringing a psychic into their home. The psychics she met at conferences and that kind of thing would often lament about how children and animals could see beyond the veil, which made them susceptible to psychic phenomena. She often wondered whether they actually believed in the things they were preaching, or whether they were in the same camp as she was: *I'm in this for the money, but I'm not outwardly doing any harm. In fact, I'm helping people because the power of suggestion is a powerful thing.* She suspected that most of the people there didn't believe in the paranormal, supernatural, or whatever the fuck else they wanted to call it. They all knew it was bullshit, but nobody would openly admit to that because they'd spent their lives building careers on it.

Albert's room was at the top of the stairs and down a long slim corridor. The ceiling was low, as they typically were in houses of that age. It felt oppressive. Mrs Sawyer knocked on the door quietly before pushing it open slowly.

'Albert, honey, this is Lilith. She's here to help you.'

Albert was laid in a hospital bed, the back of which was propped up so that he was in a sitting position. The bed was far too big to have come down the corridor they'd just walked down. Mrs Sawyer glanced back at Lilith and, sensing her question, said, 'We had to bring it in through the window. Albert didn't want to sleep in the living room, so we took the window out and had it lifted in on a little crane.'

'Oh,' Lilith said. She stepped forward toward Albert. His skin was translucent. She could see blue veins crisscrossing under his skin. He was clearly a very sick child. Lilith knew from her initial interview with Mrs Sawyer that Albert was thirteen. He looked six or seven years old, at best. His cheeks were sunken. Wires emanated out from his body and a machine beeped in the corner. Lilith tried to look past all of that, to see the boy beneath the illness.

'Hi Albert, I'm Lilith,' she said, stepping closer.

'Yeah, she just said that,' Albert said, rolling his eyes. *So that was how it was going to be.*

'Your mum tells me that you've been experiencing some paranormal things?'

'My mum is a crazy bitch,' Albert said.

'Hey now,' Mrs Sawyer said, seeming to shrink into the corner of the room. She turned to Lilith. 'I'm sorry, he wasn't like this before he got ill. He's angry.'

'No shit! Of course I'm fucking angry. I have weeks left, at best. The chemo hasn't worked. Radiotherapy hasn't worked. None of it worked. I'm done. I'm as good as dead, and I wish you'd just let me die in peace. Instead, you bring this bimbo to try and exorcise me.'

'I'm not an exorcist,' Lilith said. 'Do I look like an exorcist?' She smiled what she hoped was a cheeky smile. Teenage boys tended to like her. Objectively speaking, she was hot.

'No. I suppose not. Exorcists tend to wear more clothes.'

Lilith quickly scanned her outfit. It was her typical outfit. Leggings, a sports bra, and a nice jumper. She caught Albert's eyes trailing down her legs. It made her feel naked.

'Your mum told you why I'm here,' Lilith said, pushing through the discomfort. He was a kid, a dying kid. If anybody got a free pass, he did.

'She thinks I'm talking to my dead dad, and to an imaginary friend. I told her it's just the drugs making me see things, and hear things, but she doesn't believe me.' He stared pointedly at his mum while he spoke.

'But you know things that you couldn't possibly know. Hallucinations come from your mind, anything it says, you have to already know,' Lilith said, raising her eyebrow in question.

'Yeah, the ghost of my dear dead daddy told me that my mum fucked a priest before she married him. That makes sense, doesn't it? I couldn't possibly have gotten that information from anywhere else.'

Mrs Sawyer's hands began visibly shaking. 'I never told anybody.' She shook her head, over and over, tiny little shakes.

'Are you sure?' Albert's face was cocksure, evil.

Lilith tried to keep an easy expression on her face. It was always the prim and proper ladies who had a dark side.

'I'm sure,' Mrs Sawyer said, directing her answer to Lilith. 'He also knew that my grandfather had another family during the war. He was stationed in Japan and created a whole life there. He abandoned them and came back here after the war ended. The woman, the mother of his other children, killed herself. We found out through a friend of his who stayed there. Nobody spoke of it. Nobody. There's no way he could have known, but my husband knew that. Albert has to be speaking with him. There's no other way he could have known.'

'There's no way I could have figured out the family gossip on my own? People talk. Grandma could have told me. Aunt Maggie. And yet you're convinced a ghost told me.'

'That's not all,' Mrs Sawyer said. Her voice was barely a whisper. 'He knew about my…' she paused, a sob escaping from her mouth, '... he knew about my abortion. I never told a soul.'

Lilith watched Albert's face twist into a smirk. 'You're right. There's no way I could have known that. Shit, you caught me. You're right.' He stopped speaking and looked into the corner of the room, over Lilith's shoulder. He blinked twice and his brow furrowed. 'You want me to tell them the truth?'

Instinctually, Lilith turned in the direction Albert was looking. There was nothing there. His eyes were fixed on the coving in the corner of the ceiling.

'Who are you talking to?' Mrs Sawyer said. Her voice shook. 'Is it Nicolas or your dad?' She turned to Lilith. 'Can you just send them into the light please? Like you did with the others.'

Albert scoffed. 'She can't do anything because she's a fake. If she was real, she'd be shitting herself right now.'

'I assure you, I'm not a fake,' Lilith said. She looked to Mrs Sawyer. 'What was your husband's name?'

'Daniel,' Mrs Sawyer said.

'Daniel,' Lilith said into the room. 'I need you to go into the light. You don't belong here. It's time to move on.

'You're not even looking at him,' Albert said, smirking. He laughed, it was hacking and sickly. He paused as though he was listening to something. He squinted, nodded, and said, 'He wants you to know his real name now. He wants you to know so that when he lets you die, you'll know who to thank.'

The air left the room. Mrs Sawyer collapsed to her knees, a wail escaping her mouth.

'Can you do something? Can you get rid of it?' She directed her questions at Lilith, but didn't look up from the floor.

'Yes, of course,' Lilith said. She was thoroughly creeped out by Albert's words, but it was nothing she hadn't seen before. Kids did this all the time, usually after watching scary movies at friend's sleepovers. They scared themselves, and began to believe that they were truly haunted. The abortion thing, Lilith couldn't quite explain but there had to be a reasonable explanation. Maybe he was trying to hurt his mother and started throwing shit at the wall, seeing what stuck. It wasn't unusual for women her age to have had abortions and not talk about them.

'His name is Nicolas Damont. And he's here for me.'

'What are you talking about?' Mrs Sawyer said, crawling towards her son's bedside.

'It's your fault, you know?' Albert looked down at his mum.

'You should have protected me. If you protected me, Nicolas wouldn't have to take me away. He never preyed on children who were loved, who were protected. He only ever fed on the neglected.' He threw his head back and laughed aloud, his jaw so wide that it looked fit to snap. 'Do you know what he did to them? He lured them off the streets and into his shop. He made them feel things they'd never felt before. Then he slit their throats, chopped them up into teeny tiny pieces, and ate them.'

The subtle shift in his voice was almost imperceptible, a rough estimation of the demons you heard in movies. Lilith had to give him credit. It was theatrical. The backstory was disconcerting, as was calling a 'demon' by a human name. What kind of a demonic name was Nicolas Damont?

'Sometimes, he didn't even bother to cook them first.' The smile on his face chilled Lilith to the bone. 'He knows things about you. He knows what you did. The old ones always do. They're powerful. They can make you see things, hear things, they can sift through your memories without you ever even knowing. He says you cheated him out of a meal.'

'What are you talking about?' Mrs Sawyer screamed; each word sounded like it ripped her throat in two.

Albert tilted his head, ignoring his mum and focusing on Lilith. 'You were too drunk to be driving.'

Freezing cold fingers trailed down Lilith's spine. Her limbs shook uncontrollably. There was no way this boy could know what she did. No way. He was bluffing, just like he had done with his mother.

Lilith's breath caught in her throat.

'You were too drunk to be pregnant, to be fair, but that didn't stop you.'

The room began to spin around her.

'Did you want to kill yourself? Is that what you were trying to do? Nicolas says that you were, but you don't seem the type to kill yourself. Maybe you just wanted to kill the baby. Why else would you have been drunk, pregnant, and driving a car? It seems like the two of you have something in common. You both like to kill children.'

'How?' Lilith said. Her voice sounded like a prayer. This couldn't be real.

'Your baby would have tasted delicious,' he said. The voice was so far removed from what Albert had initially sounded like that it left no doubt in Lilith's mind that something was using Albert's mouth to speak.

Lilith shut her eyes tightly, trying to block out the scene. Trying to think reasonably. The car crash had been mentioned on Facebook and local newsgroups. She went by a different name now, but still, it didn't take a genius to link her to that. But the pregnancy was different. The pregnancy had been a secret. The crash caused her to go into labour on the dazed walk home. She buried the baby in the back garden. Her parents never knew. Never asked. Nobody else had been hurt. That had been the end of it.

'He wants you. You owe him.'

'Why?' Lilith said.

'Why what?' Albert said.

'Why me? I'm not the only one to have done what I did, so why me?'

Albert stopped and stared into the corner of the ceiling. He nodded his head slowly, and bit down on his lip hard, a smirk still peeking through. 'The reasons are twofold,' Albert said. The words were jarring from a teenager's mouth, but Lilith suspected it wasn't the teenager she was speaking to. 'First, he wanted to eat your baby so much. He would have waited until it was older though. There's not enough meat on babies.' Albert pursed his lips and pouted. 'Second, you're useful. You understand that, surely. You're a fraud. You steal people's money and pretend to take away their demons. All of your clients are innocents. The innocents taste the best.' He stopped again, and looked into the ceiling. His eyes traced along the picture rail, following an invisible being.

'How does he know about my clients?' Lilith said, attempting to buy herself some time. Albert could have, would have, Googled her before she came. He only had to read the top few reviews on her webpage to see that most of her clients were *innocent* people suffering from unimaginable pain.

'He knows everything.'

'How? He sounds like your typical ghost? Ghosts don't know everything. Hell, ghosts can barely even lift a pencil on their own.' Lilith didn't believe in ghosts, hadn't believed in ghosts, until now. Although, she was certain that whatever Nicolas Damont was, it wasn't a ghost.

'Don't you think it's funny that you came here on the day I die? On the day we all die?'

Lilith started to back out of the room. This job wasn't worth the money. She'd refund it immediately.

'What about your dad?' Lilith said, grasping at any straw she could think of.

'What about him?' Albert's head tilted as he spoke.

'You're only talking about Nicolas now. What about your dad? Where is he?'

'You stupid bitch. My dad was never here. It was always Nicolas. He likes to play with his food.'

'I can't be here. I'm sorry,' Lilith said, choking on the words. Her reptilian brain had finally kicked in, she needed to run.

'I thought you said ghosts weren't powerful. Why are you scared of Nicolas if he's not powerful?' The voice was sickly sweet, teasing her.

Lilith's words caught in her throat. She couldn't stay any longer. She had to leave.

'You can't leave. Please don't leave,' Mrs Sawyer said.

'Yes, don't leave. We're just getting to know each other. Nicolas thinks that the two of you could have a mutually beneficial relationship. A symbiosis, if you will.'

Lilith turned and ran, there was no way on this planet that he was staying there with that creepy kid. The door slammed closed in her face.

'What the fuck? Let me out!'

'Ah, so you believe now? See, Nicolas, we did it. We have ourselves a believer.'

Lilith pulled on the door handle. It wouldn't move. 'Please please please,' she said under her breath.

She turned back around, to plead with Albert. 'Let me go, please let me go.'

Albert shifted slightly in his bed before ripping all of the tubes out of his body, one by one. He flipped his legs over the edge of the bed and stood up. His shoulders drooped, and his head lolled to the side. Something was holding him up, like a puppet. There was no way a boy with so little strength was standing on his own.

'Don't worry. It's not your turn just yet. It's my turn first.' He grabbed a pen off his bedside table, 'I don't want to,' the pitch of his voice shifted significantly. He sounded like a teenage boy again. 'Don't make me, please don't make me. I thought we-'. He jammed the pen into his neck. Nothing happened for a moment, and then he yanked the pen out, throwing it to the side. Blood spurted from the gash torn into his flesh. The smile on his face never faltered as he fell to the ground.

'My baby, my boy,' Mrs Sawyer said, scrambling across the room and throwing herself onto his body. Great wracking sobs shook her as she murmured to her son.

Lilith stood, frozen to the spot. She couldn't move.

Eventually, Mrs Sawyer stilled.

'Mrs Sawyer?' Lilith said. 'What do I do? Should I phone an ambulance?'

'You need to leave, now,' she said. 'Don't come back. Don't tell anybody you were here. I'll fix this. I have to. I'm his mother.' Her head snapped to the side, her eyes widened. 'Yes, I know what I have to do.'

Lilith stumbled backward. She couldn't grasp a train of thought that made sense. She should phone an ambulance, she knew that. But doing so would have her name tied to this forever. A kid had killed himself during one of her cleansings, which would ruin her business. But could she even go back to her business after this? How could she go on pretending to cleanse people's homes from demons after what had just happened?

'I'm sorry. He wants you,' Mrs Sawyer said. 'I should have died first, and you ruined that for him.'

Lilith began to choke. It felt like something had crawled into her throat and blocked it completely. She couldn't breathe. She clawed at her neck, desperate for oxygen. The pressure built within her head; behind her eyes. Her vision blurred with tears.

Mrs Sawyer smiled at her, 'He says you have to let him in.'

Lilith awoke in her own bed the next morning with no recollection of how she got there. Her head banged furiously inside her skull.

'What the fuck?' she said, pressing her fingers tentatively to her temples. She had no recollection of the previous day. No recollection of the demon that had attached itself to her. No recollection of Albert stabbing himself in the neck and bleeding out with a smile on his face. The correspondence with Mrs Sawyer had been scrubbed clean from her mind. As far as Lilith was concerned, the Sawyers never existed.

Lilith decided she must have passed out from exhaustion. She'd been working very hard lately, so it made sense. She put two and two together in her mind, and made four. The mind has a funny way of making up stories to fill in the blanks. She spent the rest of the day in bed, after taking two paracetamol and downing a huge glass of water, and, that evening, when the headache had finally begun to fade, she read a Facebook post about a young boy named Albert who had killed himself in the next village over after losing a battle with cancer. It was tragic. She dropped a crying emoji on the post, and kept scrolling.

# Call Me By My Name

'My name is Nicolas Damont.'

The words seemed to come from nowhere and everywhere. It shook the room.

'Nicolas Damont?' Eli said. The look on his face matched the way Lilith was feeling perfectly. The name was vaguely familiar to her, like a dream she couldn't quite remember. 'What do you want? Why are you hurting this family?'

There was no response.

'Shit,' Eli said, shaking his head. 'What the fuck kind of demon is called Nicolas Damont? That's a people name, not a demon name.'

'I don't know. I'm Googling it,' Lilith said. In her peripheral vision, she could see Felix stroking his son's hair and holding him close. Rage burned white hot within her. How dare this thing hurt this child. Felix she wasn't the biggest fan of. But Asher, sweet, innocent Asher. The kid was going to need therapy for the rest of his life.

The first things to pop up in the search results were LinkedIn and Facebook profiles. The fourth result caught her eye. A Reddit page on the forum r/CreepyWikipedia. *'Nicolas Damont, known as the Werewolf of Chalons, Tailor of Chalons, or Demon Tailor of Chalons (died 1598) was a French man executed for murder, cannibalism, and for being a werewolf.'*

She scanned the posts and the white-hot rage turned ice cold. Nicolas Damont had been accused of luring children into his tailor shop, sexually abusing them, and then cutting their throats, before he ate them. The werewolf aspect of the story came from the rumour that he hunted for victims in the forest, at night, in the shape of a wolf. He'd been executed by being burned at the stake.

'What is it?' Eli said.

'One minute,' Lilith said, closing off the Reddit page and heading over to the Wikipedia article. It was the shortest Wikipedia page Lilith had ever seen. It essentially repeated what had been on the Reddit page, with one further detail that caused Lilith's breath to catch in her throat. *'He was said to have uttered curses and called for the Devil when he was burned.'*

'The Werewolf of Chalons,' Lilith read the name of the Wikipedia page aloud.

Above Lilith's head, a lightbulb blew. Eli's light fitting looked like a hand, five fingers spreading out from a central point. Glass rained down. Another flared brightly, casting the room in a surge of light, and then smashed. Lilith shielded her eyes and looked up. The next bulb flared, this time brighter than the previous one. The smell of burning filled the room. The two remaining bulbs left the room feeling odd, off-kilter, lighting only a small portion of it.

'Nicolas Damont was a child murderer in the 1500s,' Lilith said to Eli and Felix. She wished she didn't have to say all this in front of Asher, but she powered through. 'He lured orphans into his workshop, pretending to be a long-lost parent. He abused them, and then slit their throats. He was burned at the stake for what he did, and called out to the Devil during his final moments.'

Felix opened and closed his mouth a couple of times, reaching for something to say. He gave up and shook his head.

'This is a ghost? Not a demon? Are they different? Fuck, I'm so confused,' Eli said. He pushed his palms against his eyes. Lilith wanted to reach out for him, but thought better of it. She remained firmly planted in place.

'I don't know if they're the same thing. What even is a demon? We use the word all the time, right? To mean something evil, something sentient that isn't human or animal. But what is it?'

'Google it then,' Eli said.

'Because Google is a trustworthy source of information,' Lilith shook her head. 'Should I call Emmanuel?'

'Because he's a trustworthy source of information,' Eli said. The sarcasm dripped from his words like poison.

'He's the best we've got.'

'He hasn't answered any of your calls yet, but he'll answer your messages. That should tell you everything. He's Googling the answers too, why not cut out the middleman.'

Lilith considered it for a moment before trying to call Emmanuel. He'd told her to ask the demon its name, and it had got them a little further along (whether in the right direction or wrong, she wasn't sure). It rang, and rang, and rang. And then the call dropped.

A message popped on her screen. *What?*

Lilith sent a voice message, repeating what they'd found out.

She watched the three dots move around in their bubble, showing that Emmanuel was typing. She gripped the phone tighter than she ever had.

'Demons are evil spirits. The theory is that most spirits pass on to the next life shortly after death. Some stay around for a while, but then move on. Some spirits are evil: those of people who have done terrible things.' She read aloud from the message, into the eager silence of the room. 'These spirits become demons, or evil spirits. If they choose not to move on to the next plane of existence, they become stronger and stronger, and become less *spirit-like*. They lose whatever humanity they have and become demons. Many continue to commit the hateful acts they did when they were alive.'

'How the fuck could he possibly know that?' Eli asked.

'But then I should be able to see him,' Felix said. The brothers wore matching facial expressions, expressions that broke Lilith's heart. They were terrified.

'Give me a second?' Lilith said.

*How do you know that?* She typed back.

The three dots popped up.

*Can't you just answer the phone?* Lilith furiously tapped back while waiting for the answer.

The message tone chimed, and Lilith read aloud, 'We don't know this for sure. It is a very strong theory based on an abundance of research. I'd be happy to share the journal articles with you some *other time.*' Lilith could sense the sarcasm in his words, but pushed past it. 'Many *demons* that we've experienced have given names that are/were real people in history, people who committed heinous acts. Even when we think of the typical names that demons give, Abalam, Azazel, Abaddon, Baal, Belial, Lilith, Mammon, all these are named in various Biblical texts, and all of whom did terrible things in these texts. It could be a coincidence. It could be demonic creatures grasping at religious straws, finding names that we associate with evil, but I don't believe this to be the case. Records of demonic possession, of exorcism, always name the demon. The demon always has a name. Names are something inherently human. If you ask me, I'd say the evidence that demons were once human is overwhelming.'

'He's guessing,' Felix said.

'His guess is the best information we have,' Lilith said.

'Okay then,' Felix said, 'Nicolas Damont, what do you want with my family? What do you want from us?'

'I want your son,' the voice was non-directional. It came from everywhere at once. 'But he'll taste better as an orphan. Or, better yet, maybe I'll taste him through your mouth.'

A ragged, desperate cry filled the space. Felix pushed Asher to the ground and threw himself away from the child. Asher began to cry silent, confused tears. Eli knelt down next to Asher, and snaked his arms around him. He pressed the child's head to his chest, shushing quietly, and staring daggers at his brother.

'What the fuck?' Eli snarled.

Felix looked broken. His body was crumpled like a used tissue. He blinked slowly, as though waking up. His eyes sent ice trailing down Lilith's spine. They were dead, cold. Felix was no longer behind those eyes, she knew.

Specs edged forward, putting himself between Asher and Eli, and Felix. His hackles raised, and he released a slow growl of warning.

Felix pulled himself to his feet, standing tall above his brother and son. He seemed to have grown multiple feet in a matter of seconds. His face was blank; expressionless. And then his face split into a wide smile.

# Down Boy

Acting on pure instinct, Lilith grabbed hold of Specs's collar and attempted to pull him away from the thing that wasn't Felix. *Nicolas Damont.*

The dog turned and snapped at her, baring teeth. Saliva spilled from Specs's mouth. Snatching her hand back, Lilith took stock of the situation. Eli held Asher tightly to him, and Asher sobbed into his chest. Eli caught Lilith's eye and shook his head. They were fucked. They both knew it.

Felix stood, statue-still, his head tilted to the side. The smile turned Lilith's inside to jelly. It made her feel physically sick.

'Why Asher? Why not any other child?' Lilith said. She felt shitty, attempting to bargain one child's life with another.

'Lilith, you should know that better than anyone, you brought me here.' The voice from Felix's mouth wasn't his own. She could detect the faint hint of a French lilt to the words.

'I didn't do that. I didn't. I wouldn't know how,' Lilith said.

'We've met before.' Felix bit his lip as though he was being cheeky.

'What are you talking about?' Lilith pleaded.

'Albert Sawyer.' Felix said the name as though Lilith was supposed to know who it was. 'You killed him too. Remember?'

The memories of the day flooded back to her. She *did* remember. She remembered everything. A lump the size of a golf ball formed in her throat. The pressure of tears behind her eyes was agony. How had she forgotten that?

'How? Why?' she managed to stutter.

'What's happening? What does he mean?' Eli said. The words barely penetrated Lilith's consciousness.

'The moment I met you, I knew how useful you'd be,' Nicolas Damont said through Felix.

Lilith wasn't sure how she remained standing. Her entire body went weak.

'I saw who you were, what you did. You're a charlatan, a fraud. You prey on the weak, the needy, the vulnerable. We're the same, you and I. Kindred spirits. You didn't even know that I was a part of you. I made you forget Albert. And then I lay in wait just below the surface, waiting for my next target, and you brought me the perfect victim. As soon as you walked into this home, I knew you hadn't let me down. The child is just my type, but you know that now. You know who I am, what I did, what I intend to do to him.'

Flashbacks of the memories Damont made her forget - of Albert Sawyer stabbing the pen in his throat - tore through her. She wouldn't allow that to happen again.

'No, you can't have him. I won't let you.'

'What is he talking about?' Eli shouted. Lilith glanced in his direction and saw Asher peeking from his uncle's shirt.

'I… I don't know how to…' Lilith said. How could she possibly explain to Eli that they'd been right all along? That she had brought the demon here. That it was her fault. That all of this was her fault.

Felix stepped towards her. She stepped back. Specs remained in place, protecting Asher from the thing that used to be his father. Specs's stance showed he was ready to attack. He was hunched forward, over his front legs, a tightly wound coil ready to unfurl.

The room plunged into darkness. Specs erupted into feral barks. It was darkness like nothing Lilith had ever experienced. Complete and utter darkness. She couldn't hear anything except for Specs. His barks became unhinged, panicked.

She felt exposed and began to slowly edge backward towards the wall. She knew it was some primal instinct that forced her to do this. The instinct to stay alive, to protect herself from at least one angle.

'Asher? Asher?' Eli's panicked voice came from the darkness, only just louder than Specs's incessant barking.

The light snapped back on. Although only one bulb now remained in the fixture, the light was blinding. Lilith blinked against it.

'Where's Asher? Asher!' Eli screamed.

Asher and Felix had vanished from the room.

Specs whined, an agonising, desperate noise.

Lilith didn't wait. She ran.

# It's In Me

When the demon had slipped inside him, wearing him like a glove, he'd felt it. His thoughts no longer controlled his body. Felix was trapped. His body was out of his control. He stared through his own eyes and watched the demon use him like a puppet. He fought against it with everything he had. It was agonising. Each step, each gesture, Felix fought. The sensation of trying to stop the demon burned white hot, but he would never stop fighting.

Felix's mouth moved, words were said that weren't his own. He watched his son sob against Eli's chest and he could do nothing to comfort him.

The memories were torture. Nicolas Damont sent them to torture him, there was no doubt in Felix's mind about that. There was nothing he could do to stop them. They played across his mind as though they were really happening in front of him. Flashes of young boys, their throats slit, blood dribbling down their naked torsos; the rancid iron scent clawing at his throat. Flashes of him butchering them. Cutting meat off their body and slipping it into his mouth. Felix could taste the raw human flesh. The slippery texture caused bile to build in his neck while the meat slid down into his stomach.

*Please stop.* Felix screamed.

*Wait until you see what I have planned for your son.* The words were inside his brain. They hadn't been spoken aloud.

He listened as his mouth spoke to Lilith. He felt the surge of power as the light was sucked out of the room. He felt his body, with a speed beyond his human capabilities, snatch Asher out of Eli's arms, and run upstairs. Nicolas Damont was toying with his meal. The thought would have caused Felix to collapse to the ground if he'd been in control of his own body.

He tried to stop the *thing* controlling him from throwing Asher across his bedroom. He tried with every fibre of his being. The sensation of the demon inside him using his body like a fucked-up marionette puppet felt like knife slices against his mind.

All he could do was watch as Nicolas Damont tortured his son. Asher's screams pierced his heart. The demon wouldn't allow him to look away. Felix watched as Nicolas Damont conjured fire and burned Asher's skin to a crisp. He picked up Asher's body and threw it against the wall, without using his hands, and did this repeatedly until the boy fell unconscious. It was a small mercy, that his son was no longer aware of the torture he was being subjected to.

When Lilith barged into the room, the feeling of relief overwhelmed Felix.

Her mouth dropped open and she ran across the room to his son.

*Do you recognise the injuries?* Nicolas Damont said inside Felix's head. Felix was aware that he was allowing Lilith to approach Asher. The demon could have easily stopped her if he wanted to.

*Jenna.* She'd not been wearing her seatbelt. She'd dropped something in the footwell and was leaning over to pick it up when her car was T-boned, and sent careening into a ditch at the side of the road. There had been a petrol leak. A spark. And she'd burned alive.

Asher's injuries mirrored those of his mother.

*Correct.* Nicolas Damont said, maniacal laughter filling Felix's head.

The cacophony of laughter was so overwhelming that he barely registered Eli and Specs entering the room. He barely registered Specs's low growl. Barely registered Eli grabbing hold of his collar and shaking him; saying words he couldn't quite grasp.

The laughter rang around inside his head as he stared into Eli's eyes, trying to communicate with his brother, trying to explain that this wasn't him, it was Nicolas Damont.

The laughing ceased and his world went silent.

'Felix,' Eli repeated, over and over again, holding him by the collar and shaking him violently. Felix wasn't allowed to respond. He tried, but his mouth wouldn't form the words. The demon was in control of him. Eli and Lilith needed to get Asher as far away from him as possible. Asher was in danger. If Nicolas got his way, he'd turn Asher into one of his victims, and Felix could do nothing to stop him. Nicolas would use Felix's hands to kill and eat his son.

'Get him out of here,' Eli said to Lilith. She nodded, scooped Asher up, and carried him like a babe out of the room.

Nicolas Damont let her.

Felix wouldn't allow himself to feel relieved. If Damont was allowing Lilith to take away Asher, *his target, his meal,* then there had to be an ulterior motive for that.

Felix's body stepped toward Eli. They stood nose to nose.

'I know this isn't you, Felix. I know it's him.'

Felix's arms shot out, his hands meeting Eli's chest, and pushing him backwards. The power that came from his body was impossible. Eli's back hit the wall, several feet behind him, and he crumpled to the floor.

'Fuck,' Eli snarled.

The voice in Felix's head laughed.

*Please don't hurt them.* Felix thought with as much force as he could.

*But it's so much fun,* the voice replied. Felix could hear the smile on his words.

*Why us? Why Asher?*

*You're asking what makes you special? Why are humans always so obsessed with being special?* Felix heard the words as clearly as if they'd been spoken aloud. Nicolas Damont's accent rounded out each of the words.

*Why us? Why my family?*

*Because your trauma is delicious. I can smell it on Asher. The ones without parents always taste exquisite. Their suffering tenderises the meat. One dead parent is fine; two is a delicacy.*

If Felix would have been in charge of his own body, he would have been sick. Instead, he sensed saliva filling his mouth at the prospect of a 'delicious meal'.

*Please don't hurt him. Take me instead.*

*I don't want you!* The words boomed inside his mind. *I want the boy. All those years of suffering, of living without his mother, has made him ripe for the picking and YOU brought me straight to him. You, in your delusion, thinking that you had the right, the purpose, to make the world aware of Lilith's schemes. Your sense of self-righteousness brought me here.*

'Felix,' Eli mumbled. He leaned against the wall, hand against his head. The second concussion in a day, Felix realised. His brother would be in agony.

Felix's body stood. He watched his brother try to stand on drunken legs, pitching forward and landing on his hands and knees.

'Felix, you can fight him. Don't let him win.'

*I CAN'T*, Felix screamed.

*No, you can't,* Damont said.

*How are you doing this?* Felix asked. The spirits he'd seen over the years couldn't interact with their surroundings at all. They couldn't flick a light switch, hide your car keys, move your favourite pen. But Nicolas Damont had *possessed* him. Amongst all the other things he'd done, he'd POSSESSED him. Spirits shouldn't be able to do that.

*Oh, you sweet naïve boy,* Damont said. *This is what happens when you refuse to pass over. Why would anybody want to leave this plane of existence? In my human body, I ate for sustenance, for pleasure. Here, I eat to grow stronger. I suck the life out of my victims until they have no other option but to end their pathetic little lives. I don't even miss their meat anymore, because their trauma tastes so good. Their spirits taste so good.*

*You eat their spirits?* Felix thought. He was glad he didn't have to say the words aloud because he wasn't sure he'd have had the energy to do so.

*Oh yes, and I'm not the only one. There are many of us. We feast on the recently deceased. We all have different preferences, mind, so there's no overlap. I like little boys, sad little boys. Others might like young women who died in car accidents, for example.*

*Oh God,* Felix thought. Jenna. He'd never seen her spirit. He hoped that she'd moved straight on.

*I heard that she was delightfully tender,* Damont said.

Felix felt the blood rush to his head, nausea overcame him, but his body remained upright.

Eli pulled himself to his feet using the dressing table to hold himself up.

'Felix, Felix, please, come back,' Eli pleaded. Blood oozed from a wound at the back of his head. He looked drunk, swaying on the spot, reaching out with a hand toward Felix.

Felix felt his face contort into a smile. His feet began to move. He walked straight past Eli and out of the bedroom door in search of Asher and Lilith. Specs nipped at his heels, grabbing hold of the back of his jeans and trying to pull him back. He shook the dog off with ease, but Specs didn't let up. He snarled, and bit, and pulled. Pain bloomed in Felix's ankles, but his body continued to walk forward, making the slow descent toward the kitchen, toward his son.

# This Isn't Me

The knife felt cold in Felix's hand. His fingers gripped it against their will. He tried to peel them open, to let it drop to the floor, but his body wouldn't listen to him. Each movement the demon made against Felix's will burned. It was agonising. He continued to fight with the remainder of his dwindling strength.

He could hear Lilith speaking to Asher in hushed words, trying to calm him. Asher's sobs shook the house and tore at Felix's heart.

Specs's teeth clamped, once again, onto Felix's calf. The pain was searing, unbearable. Damont ignored it, and forced Felix onwards, towards the living room.

'No,' Eli said, throwing himself down the hallway, bumping off walls and furniture. The blood had turned one half of his white shirt brown. He threw himself at Felix, whose arm swiped him away with little effort. Eli's head slammed against the sideboard and he slid to the floor, unmoving.

*No no no no no,* Felix repeated the word like a prayer.

*I could make you do anything, you realise that, right? I'm going to make you slit your son's throat, cut his flesh from the bone, and eat it raw and you won't be able to do anything about it.*

*Please don't. Please no.* Felix had nothing left to give, there was nothing left to do except plead.

*But first, Lilith. The things I could make you do to her.*

Images filled Felix's mind. He couldn't close his eyes against them. Felix raping Lilith as she pleaded for him to stop. Felix taking the knife he held in his hand and peeling the skin off her bones like he was peeling an apple. Felix taking the knife to her throat and hacking and hacking until her head fell with a dull thud to the floor, separated from her body.

*But it's not Lilith that worries you, is it? You're worried about what I'll make you do to your own son. You're worried you'll enjoy it, just like I do. There's no better feeling than holding the life of an innocent in your bare hands, of doing whatever you want with them… whatever you want. Then holding their shaking, spasming body as their spirit leaves. You asked me why, why your family, why I chose this life? I get the best of both worlds. I get to live the life I always wanted to, without fear of persecution, using your body, or the body of whoever else, to enact my plans, and then I get to eat the sweet, innocent, tortured souls. The worst part for you is that I wouldn't even let you die. I'd make you stay alive to face the police, the public, yourself. You'd have to live with the memories of what you did forever. I will taste him through your mouth and you'll be cursed with those memories for the rest of your sad little life.*

Specs tore a chunk out of Felix's leg in a failed attempt at stopping him from stepping into the living room. Damont didn't flinch. He walked as though nothing had happened, as though Specs hadn't latched back onto Felix's leg.

Felix tried to stop his legs from moving. He tried harder than he'd tried anything in his life. The pain of trying to prevent Damont from using his body as a puppet was excruciating.

When he saw Asher, curled up against Lilith's chest, great sobs wracking his body, his heart broke into two.

*FUCKING STOP,* he snarled, knowing that only Damont could hear his voice. Felix's body walked towards them.

'Felix, what's happening?' Lilith's face changed as understanding washed over her. Her eyes lowered to his hand, to the knife. 'Stay there. Don't come closer.'

*Please please don't hurt him. I'll do anything, please.*

Lilith stood, pushing Asher behind her. 'Stay back,' she said.

A rush of gratitude flooded Felix's system. Lilith was protecting Asher. Given her track record, Felix had fully expected her to run, to abandon them and leave them to Damont's hand. Yet, against all odds, she'd stayed.

Specs ripped the back off Felix's right knee, pulling a chunk of skin and gore free and sending Felix careening to the floor.

*Kill me, Specs. Just kill me,* Felix thought.

His body spun to look at Specs who stood his ground, blood covering his maw. He looked fierce. *Do it, Specs. Kill me,* Felix begged.

# Upon Which It Feeds

Lilith lunged for the knife. It was an instinctual reaction. She had no time to think about the consequences.

*Kill the host, kill the demon.* The words were a prayer.

Felix knelt like he was proposing, kneeling on the leg that was missing the entire back of his knee. It wasn't Felix. She knew that. It was Nicolas Damont. Damont stared down Specs, reaching out with both hands towards the frenzied dog.

The only way to kill Damont was to kill Felix too. *Kill the host, kill the demon.*

The knife was warm, slick with sweat, as she plunged it towards the side of Felix's neck.

'NO!' Damont said, flinging the word from Felix's mouth. Without Felix touching her, she was thrown across the room, landing like a ragdoll. The knife fell from her hand, clattering onto the floor. She couldn't see where it had landed. She had failed.

Asher remained in place at the other side of the room.

'I'm so sorry,' she said to him. He was no longer sobbing. Instead, tears tracked down his face lazily, like he'd resigned himself to his fate.

Felix pulled himself to standing, balancing on his intact leg.

'You bitch,' he snarled. He walked toward her slowly, dragging his wounded leg behind him. It reminded her of zombies from The Night of the Living Dead, not that she liked horror films. Specs continued to attack, biting and ripping, trying to stop Felix from reaching Lilith. His attempts were futile, Damont would use Felix's body until it was completely incapacitated.

'Run. Leave. Now,' Lilith said to Asher, a last-ditch attempt at saving the kid's life for just a little longer. Damont would catch up with him eventually.

Felix's eyes were fixed on Lilith. Damont's smile tugged at his lips. Lilith refused to look away. She wouldn't cower. She would face the demon head-on. His hands clamped around her neck, picking her up from the floor. Lilith's sight began to blur. In her peripheral vision, she caught Asher moving. Picking up the knife, and stepping toward Felix. He thrust the knife into Felix's side. His hands relaxed, dropping Lilith to the floor.

Damont spun around and dove for Asher. The knife fell from his little hand as Damont grabbed him by the shoulders, shaking him violently.

This was her chance. Her only chance.

The knife was slippery with Felix's blood. She could barely grip it.

The neck. She had to kill him. Felix's death was the only way to get rid of Damont.

Felix continued to shake Asher. Lilith moved swiftly, bringing the knife up in an arc, and plunging it into Felix's neck.

'I'm sorry Felix, I'm sorry.' The knife struck bone and stuck. It took all her strength to pull it free.

Asher fell to the floor and sat there dazed. Blood spurted from Felix's neck in intervals. Their eyes met as he fell to the floor. They were wet with unshed tears. She could see Felix in them once more.

'Oh my god, no,' Eli said. Lilith hadn't seen him enter the room. Black blood crusted the right side of his face.

He lurched forward, and collapsed next to Felix. He placed his hands against the knife wound in his neck. Blood continued to pulse through his fingers.

'He needs to die,' Lilith said.

Eli looked up at Lilith, eyes pleading with her. 'He's my brother.'

'That wasn't your brother. Kill the host, kill the demon.' Her voice sounded like stone, void of any emotion. She wasn't sure how that was possible, given what she'd just experienced, but she felt nothing.

'Daddy?'

Asher. Lilith had almost forgotten that he was there. That he'd just witnessed his dad's murder, at her hand. He sat cross-legged on the floor, allowing Specs to lick the tears off his face. One hand trailed up and down Specs's back.

Eli released Felix's neck and crawled over to Asher. He wrapped his arms around the boy. Lilith watched as Asher's shoulders shook.

'I'm going to phone the police,' Lilith said. Neither of them reacted.

She pulled her phone out of her pocket and dialed 999. It wasn't until she was through to the operator that she realised she didn't know what to say.

# DON'T LIE

'I killed a man. We need an ambulance and the police,' Lilith said into the phone. The operator had asked her question after question, none of which she answered, she couldn't think quickly enough, and so she hung up the phone and went back to Eli and Asher. She corralled them into the kitchen. Asher shouldn't be around his dad's mutilated body. It didn't look good.

'What the fuck are we going to tell the police?' Eli said. He didn't bother to glance apologetically at Asher for his language. There was no point anymore.

Lilith attempted to gather her thoughts, to mould them into something resembling intelligent thought. There was only one way to play it as far as she could tell. Only one way for Asher to have a shot at a decent life.

'The truth,' she said. 'I'll tell them the truth, or stick as closely to it as possible. We'll have to say that Felix had a mental breakdown, started seeing things, and tried to kill his own son.' The words felt like razor blades in her throat.

'But-' Eli said.

'No, we have to do this. Asher needs you to be around, so we have to make this as easy for them as possible. You need to tell them the truth about Felix. It will paint him in a bad light, but I can't see another way around it. I mean, who would believe us? Who would believe what actually happened?

Eli placed his hands on the table, his shoulders hunched over. 'People will hate him.'

Lilith knew that '*people*' was the whole world. The world would see a man who suffered a tragic loss and didn't receive treatment, was triggered by a fraudulent psychic, had a mental breakdown, and tried to kill his son. Lilith would be able to claim self-defence, maybe, but that left a pit of acid in her stomach. This was all her fault, and Felix would be remembered as the English lecturer who snapped and tried to murder a psychic, and his family. She should have died, not him. That would have been a better ending.

'People will forgive him. He'll be labelled as an undiagnosed schizophrenic or something. Hearing voices, seeing things, it fits the bill. Most people think paranormal activity is just mental illness anyway. I sure as hell did until today. So just tell them the truth,' Lilith repeated. 'Leave the bits out of *you* witnessing actual demonic activity. Let them think he was insane. You're Asher's only family. If you tell them what actually happened, they'll take him away.'

'What about me?' Asher asked.

'You tell them the truth. They'll say you were imagining things. They don't believe little kids, Asher.'

He nodded, like an adult who'd been tasked with a great responsibility. Tears continued to fall silently down his face. He sporadically wiped at them with the sleeve of his shirt.

The blue lights lit up the windows, casting the room in an eerie glow.

'I really am sorry. I didn't mean for this to happen. I wish I could take it back,' Lilith said.

Eli shrugged. 'You couldn't have known this would happen.' He lowered his voice, 'Do you think Nicolas Damont is really gone?'

'I hope so. I really fucking do,' Lilith said.

# Us Against the World

Eli and Asher spent the next twenty-four hours at the police station. The police had attempted to take Specs into their police kennels but Eli had threatened them with legal action if the dog was touched. Instead, Specs had been photographed, swabbed, and released to Mrs Birch's care until Eli was released. As she walked Specs to her house, Eli heard her telling the dog he'd be getting a *nice bath.* Against all odds, that made him smile.

Eli told his version of the truth, gave a verbal and written statement, and was given a once-over by the station's duty nurse. He said the things he needed to say to keep Asher safe, even if it meant throwing his brother to the wolves. Felix would have told him to do it, he knew, but it still left a foul taste in his mouth.

Asher was interviewed with an *appropriate adult* in the room, since Eli was busy being interviewed himself. After they'd been picked over by crime scene people, and photographed, they'd been allowed to shower and had been given grey tracksuits to wear. They looked like they'd been released from prison, but it was better than the clothes they'd been wearing, crusted over with blood.

All Eli wanted to do was go to bed, with Asher and Specs by his side. He was told that he needed to be reachable, and that Felix's body would be released when the pathologists and coroners had finished with him. Eli tried not to think of his brother's body, slit from neck to groin, and splayed open like a butterfly on a slab, huge chunks of meat missing thanks to Specs who, until that moment, had never hurt a fly. But the image floated around his periphery.

Eli wasn't allowed to go home because his house was still a crime scene, nor was he allowed to go to Felix's house until it had been searched and cleared. He didn't want to go to a hotel and, if he was being honest with himself, he wanted his mum.

'Shall we go see Nanna?' Eli said to Asher as they walked out of the police station. A policeman offered to take them where they needed to go. He was a young officer, clearly new to the force, and looked at them with such a huge amount of sympathy it made Eli uncomfortable.

The bags under Asher's eyes were black as coal. He nodded once.

'Come on then,' he said. He gave the officer the address and shuffled into the back of the car with Asher, holding his nephew against him. He planned to never let Asher out of his sight again.

Nobody had informed Eli's mum of Felix's death yet. Eli told the officers that he would do it in person. He hadn't wanted her to be alone when she heard. He didn't know how he was going to tell her that her son was dead. He ran through different scenarios in his mind and none of them worked. The walk along the corridor to her room took an age. Asher's hand was slick in his. He held it tightly.

When they reached her room, Eli knocked and tried the door. It wouldn't open and there was no answer. It wasn't unusual for his mum not to hear the door, but it was unusual for the door to be locked. He pulled out his keys and unlocked the door. The smell of ammonia and shit hit him instantly, like a wave.

'Stay there,' he said to Asher, over his shoulder.

Asher did as he was told and waited in the doorway while Eli walked into the flat. His mum hung from the ceiling lamp by a rope. Her neck was obviously snapped, and her nightdress was soiled.

Eli fell to his knees. He held back a scream. 'Can you go and get a nurse please Asher? And don't come in here?' he said.

He heard Asher's retreating footsteps, and managed to stand back up. A note was left on the kitchen worktop, written in his mum's neat script.

*Felix and Eli,*

*I'm so very sorry I didn't tell you the whole story. I was scared that you would stop me. I told you enough to keep you safe. I hope that neither of you are the ones to find me. But this is the only way I knew to help. Demons are spirits that have remained on our plane for too long. They thrive on hurt and pain. I felt the demon on you, Felix, when you came to see me. Once you see a demon, you know a demon. I called it back, and offered myself as a sacrifice. It readily agreed. So, this is it, I'm sorry I couldn't tell you what I planned to do. I needed to keep Asher safe, and this is the only way I know how. I've seen it work before; a life for a life. Back in my younger years I came across a demon. You can find the accounts in my diaries. I'll warn you, it doesn't make for light reading.*

*My boys, I'm sorry. I love you more than life itself, and so I go into this sacrifice readily, eagerly. I'm so proud of you.*

*All my love,*

*Mum*

Even as his mind swam, Eli knew the sacrifice made no sense. The demon, Damont, wanted young boys. It had wanted Asher. It had no use for an old woman. It wasn't the demon's type. Unless it had been toying with her, promising her that her grandson would be okay if he sacrificed herself in his place. The demon himself had all but said it: they thrive off death and destruction. What better way to ruin a family than murdering the matriarch?

The more he thought about it, the less any of it made sense to him. His family had been ripped apart because of a pretend psychic that his stupid brother had invited into their lives. His brother was now dead by her hand. His mum had killed herself in an attempt to save them all. And now his nephew would have to live with the trauma of having experienced it all. Asher was alive, the demon was dead, but at what cost?

# Epilogue – Three Months Later

The phone call was a collect call from the prison. Lilith.

Eli had done his best to put everything behind him, to come to terms with the fact that some questions would have to remain unanswered. The one thing he couldn't let go was his mum's death. She'd been an innocent party. Felix, well, Felix had brought it on himself, which caused a strange mix of emotions whenever Eli thought of his brother, which was often. But their mum, she'd sacrificed herself to try and save them. A sacrifice that made no sense. If she'd known the demon was Nicolas Damont, known what and who he wanted, then she'd have known that her sacrifice meant nothing to him. A life for a life only worked when both lives are of equal value. To Damont, child murderer and cannibal, Eli's mum was not a fair trade.

'I have a theory,' Lilith said. 'But no concrete answers. I don't think you'll ever figure this one out, Eli, I'm sorry.'

When he'd first called her, a month after that fateful day, she'd been shocked. Once he told her his concerns, she understood. She was the only person on the planet who wholeheartedly believed him, and so she was the only person he could ask questions like, 'Why would Damont agree to use my mother as a sacrifice?'

'My best theory is that Damont was toying with her. Demons like death, that much we know for certain. If an old lady threatened to hang herself as a sacrifice, what demon wouldn't enjoy that? As a bonus, if Asher found out about his grandmother's death, it would upset him greatly, right? And Asher was Damont's target. He wanted Asher to be hurt, in pain, and his grandmother hanging would definitely achieve that.'

'I should have told her what was going on. If she'd have known, she wouldn't have made a pointless sacrifice.'

'It was a Hail Mary,' Lilith said. 'A last ditch attempt to save her family. She might well have done it anyway.'

'Yeah, maybe,' Eli said. He was still unconvinced, but it was the best he was going to get.

'Eli, can I ask you something?' Lilith's voice dipped lower.

'Yeah,' he said. 'Of course.'

'Have you, ah, have you experienced anything else since what happened?'

'What do you mean?'

'You know what I mean. Haunting. Demonic activity. Have you experienced anything?'

'No, Damont is dead,' Eli said.

'What if he's not? What if killing the host didn't work?'

'What are you saying?' Eli asked.

'Things are happening here. I think he's here.'

'You killed him,' Eli said, careful of his words. The phone conversations were recorded.

'But what if that didn't work? We only had your mum's words, and Emmanuel's. Nobody knows for sure.' She paused, breathing heavily into the phone. 'I think he's here.'

**THE END.**

# BONUS CONTENT

## *A Story for Another Time – The Diary of Clara Eastwood*

**6th April, 1970.**

Dad still isn't right. It's been weeks since Karen left him, and he's still moping around the house. He goes to work, digs the graves, and comes home. He stinks of sweat and soil, and he doesn't shower. I try to convince him, but he refuses. I talked to Richard about it and he says my dad is depressed. That Karen cheating on him with the guy who runs the gym made him depressed. I don't understand why though. Karen was a bitch. I'm glad she's not here anymore.

**7th April, 1970.**

He's still ignoring the spirits, which means they're coming to me instead. I don't have the time to deal with them all, what with applying for Sixth Form and trying to get through my O Levels. He's not helping them, so I have to. What else can I do? Ignore them? Then they'd stick around for longer. It's just annoying that I have to be the one to see them to the other side, if they need some gentle coaxing. I didn't choose to live next to the church and graveyard. Dad did. He thought it would make it easier to help the spirits along, just as my Grandma Nell had done when she was alive. He saw it as his calling. I saw it as an annoyance that I'd rather be without. I already get called Ghost Girl because I, stupidly, admitted at a sleepover when I was ten that I could see spirits. It's hard enough living a normal life without having to pick up my dad's slack too.

**8th April, 1970.**

It's the Easter holidays and I'm bored stiff. My friends are on holiday. We never go on holiday. Ever. Dad says that we're needed here. It's probably one of the reasons Karen left him. She was forever talking about the places she'd been before she met Dad. He told me today that he'd told her he could see spirits, and that's why she left. I'm not so sure I believe that. If you love somebody, you believe them when they're telling you their truth. He cried for ages afterward. I didn't know what to do. I just sat with him and rubbed his back like he did when Jimmy Gordon dumped me for Marissa Johnston.

**9th April, 1970.**

I met somebody today. There were no graves to be dug, so Dad was tending to the graveyard. I sat with my back against the grave of Old Mrs Specter. She was a spiteful old bat in real life, so I feel completely at ease using her grave as a seat. A young boy walked over to me. I didn't see him until he blocked the sun and made it so I couldn't see the words in my book, *Something Wicked This Way Comes.* I looked up and immediately flushed. I hate that my cheeks do that when I'm nervous. The boy was gorgeous. Dark hair. The brightest blue eyes you've ever seen. He was a bit older than me, eighteen, he said. His parents had moved him to the area so that his dad could work in a local mine. The mine he'd worked in had closed down. *Bloody Tories.* He'd said. I'd nodded, despite not knowing what he was talking about.

Freddy Stevenson sat with me for hours. We talked about books, movies, our friends. And as the sun began to set, he walked me home. We're going to go into town tomorrow to see a movie. I can't wait.

**10th April, 1970.**

I don't remember anything that happened in the film. Freddy slipped his hand through mine ten minutes in and that was all I could think about. After the film finished, he invited me back to his house. It was one of the mining terraces a few streets over from mine, so I said yes. He asked me if I believed in ghosts. I laughed and he looked at me like I was crazy. He said that back home, he and his friends had used a Ouija board and summoned a spirit. Since then, he'd been haunted, he said. He looked like he expected me to be scared. I wasn't. I knew *ghosts.* Well, I knew spirits. A spirit/ghost is the soul, or whatever you want to call it, of a person after they die. Sometimes they stay around longer than they should and cause cold spots, things to move, but never anything crazy. I couldn't see a spirit anywhere near Freddy, so I thought he might just be lying to impress me. Maybe to trick me into snuggling up with him.

**11th April, 1970**

Something isn't right with Freddy. I spent all day with him today and he spent the whole time trying to convince me that he was haunted. I tried not to give too much away. I didn't know him well enough to tell him I can see spirits, so I just smiled and nodded like a good girl. He didn't like that. His demeanour changed. It's like he wanted me to be scared. He told me that he'd prove it. The hauntings happened at night, he said. I'm going to sneak out of my room tonight and go to his house. He says I can see the hauntings for myself.

**12th April, 1970.**

My hand is shaking so badly as I write this. I can't believe that I was stupid enough to go to Freddy's house last night. I barely know him and I just waltzed over there at 10 pm like I didn't have a care in the world. Freddy looked different. He looked unwell. He was pale anyway, but his skin was almost transparent, except for the deep bags under his eyes. When I got there, I threw a stone at his window, and he came and let me in. He told me that his parents were sleeping and to be quiet. I should have turned and walked away. I should never have walked into his home.

His bedroom was freezing cold. The window was closed tightly, so there was no reason for it to be cold. I pulled my cardigan tightly around my body but it didn't help.

'The ghost does that,' Freddy said. 'He makes it so cold that sometimes I'm scared I won't wake up.'

Goosebumps lined my skin and I almost walked away. Almost.

He told me to sit on the bed and watch.

I did.

The figure grew from nothing. The darkness in the corner of his room got thicker and thicker until it was dense blackness in the shape of a hooded figure.

I ran.

Whatever was in that room wasn't a ghost. It was something dark. Demonic.

Freddy shouted for me to come back. That it wanted me, not him. That if I let *him* (the demon) have me, it would leave Freddy alone. It didn't want Freddy. It wanted me.

**13th April, 1970.**

I told Dad what happened with Freddy. He went spare. He made me take him to Freddy's house so that he could talk to Freddy's parents. He didn't believe me when I told him about the figure in the corner of the room, I could see that. He was annoyed that an older boy had convinced me to go to his bedroom in the middle of the night, with the intention of what? Scaring me? Taking advantage of me?

There was no answer at the door. Dad pushed it open. It was the most animated I'd seen him since Karen left. He shouted inside but heard nothing. I told him again about the thing in Freddy's room. My dad ran upstairs to Freddy's room. The first thing I noticed was a note on the bed. The second, was Freddy's hanging body.

The note said *I'm sorry.*

Freddy is dead. I'm grounded. I'm not allowed to ever leave my room again.

**14th April, 1970.**

The police talked to me today. Apparently, Freddy's family still lives in Coventry. He's been missing for days. I don't know what to think. My dad won't leave my side. It's like he's scared I'm going to fall to pieces. He thinks I imagined the figure in the room. I didn't. I know what I saw. I know what I felt. It was evil. I think it killed Freddy. I see it out of the corner of my eye now. Watching over me. I asked it who it was, but Dad heard me and told me to stop making things up. The house is freezing now.

**15th April, 1970.**

The figure stood over me while I tried to sleep. I could feel it. It didn't speak. It just stood there. I refused to open my eyes, but I could hear it whispering to me. It said my name, and then it said it wanted to kill me.

**16th April, 1970.**

Dad believes me now. He saw it for himself. He dragged me to church repeating Hail Marys over and over again. He's so mad at me. He says that I've brought something evil into our lives. He sat me down in the church and told me to pray for our souls. I did, while the demon watched. Just before bed, I felt the demon slip into my skin. I could feel it reaching out inside my mind, touching my memories, feeding off the sadness, the fear. I could feel how hungry it was.

**17th April, 1970.**

I didn't get out of bed today. I could feel how desperately the demon wanted me. Dad went to work and left me alone. I'm so scared.

**18th April, 1970.**

Dad didn't go to work yesterday. He went to see the priest. Father Caplan told Dad that if a demon had attached itself to me, the only ways to get rid of it were to do an exorcism (and the church doesn't do those anymore) or wait for it to possess me, or somebody else, and then kill it. The demon laughed when it heard my dad speak. It told me it would kill me slowly so that it could feed off my suffering, before allowing itself to take my life, just before the pain became unbearable.

**30th April, 1970.**

I've only just found the strength to write again. My grief consumes every waking moment. My guilt even more so. There was a third way to get rid of the demon. One my dad didn't speak about before because he didn't want the demon to know what he knew. Sacrifice. A willing sacrifice is a powerful thing. Far more powerful than any other type of death. My dad knelt on the church's altar and slit his throat. There was a note in his back pocket. The police found it when they stripped his body for autopsy.

*My dearest Clara,*

*Please forgive me. There was another way to rid you of the demon. I couldn't tell you because then it would know what I planned to do. This was the only way. Father Caplan told me stories of demons, of what it would do to you. I couldn't let that happen to you. And so I plan to sacrifice myself. I will do it in church, allowing my blood to tarnish the altar of Christ. Demons like that, Father Caplan said, since demons are the opposite of all Christ stands for. Whether you believe in Jesus or not, it's a powerful image, my blood staining something that is supposed to represent goodness and holiness. A willing sacrifice is the third way to banish a demon. The sheer desperation of sacrificing yourself to save a loved one is a powerful thing. Demons feed off negative emotions – pain, guilt, grief, desperation. My death is, therefore, worth more than yours to the demon, according to Father Caplan. I pray to God that he is right. As I end my own life, I will say the words he told me to: I readily sacrifice myself to you. I eagerly sacrifice myself to you. I desperately sacrifice myself to you. By accepting my sacrifice, you will allow my daughter to live a life untouched by your pain and suffering. You will leave my daughter alone for the rest of her days.*

Blood covered the bottom of the letter, making it impossible to decipher. I spent every day since I was given this note by the police trying to decipher what it said.*

*The remainder of the note that Clara, unfortunately, was not able to decipher read:

*In accepting my sacrifice, your kind will never be able to feed from her again. She will be deemed untouchable to you. I sacrifice my life so that hers remains untouched.* It was what Father Caplan told Clara's father (Michael Eastwood) to say. As a member of the church, he was aware of how contractual the wording of a sacrifice had to be, in order for it to be fulfilled. Demons were sneaky, and would happily accept a sacrifice while using a loophole to continue to torment the family in question. The advice, while sound at the time, meant that Clara was unable to sacrifice herself to Nicolas Damont in the later years of her life, after her son inadvertently invited a demon into his home. Further, Nicolas Damont wouldn't have accepted Clara's sacrifice anyway. She was far too old for his tastes, even if sacrifices were far more potent than any death caused by the demon's hand. Either way, Clara's sacrifice meant nothing.

https://www.reddit.com/r/CreepyWikipedia/comments/13j
h8te/nicolas_damont_known_as_werewolf_of_ch%C3%A2lons/

# Acknowledgements

As has become tradition, I have to start by thanking the creature snoring loudly next to me as I write this (no, not my partner, Danny), my dog, Buster. Rescuing you from the shelter almost six years ago was THE BEST decision of my life. You saved me, and mean more to me than you can ever possibly know. Now, onto animals with decidedly less fur. Danny, my tech support, emotional support person, and my favourite human. He won't see this because he doesn't read books (he doesn't just avoid my books, but books in general). Thank you for being supportive AF, and for always making sure the Wi-Fi works. I couldn't do this without you. Literally. I'd have no internet.

My beta reader extraordinaires… Mum, and Auntie Julie. My books are a thousand times better thanks to your keen eye, hilarious in-line comments, and your ability to spot plot holes that I miss.

My dad, who – now he's retired – has become quite the horror reader. Thank you for everything, and I LOVE that I can now discuss books with you.

Joe, Shannon, and Alfredo. You're awesome, and your support means everything. Thank you for being friends, as well as family.

To my friends. As big-headed as it sounds, there are too many to mention them all here… You're all amazing. Special thanks to Emma, Jess, Kris, Vicki, Rachel, Jade, and James. You guys are the best. A special shout-out to my neighbours, Linzi and Gail, who push my books far better than I ever could. Sorry for the nightmares Linzi.

I have to give a massive thank you to Mary Hoyle for the proof-reading of this manuscript. I would highly recommend her (you can find her on Intsagram @mary.h.writes/ and on Fiverr – Mary_h_writes). I apologise for the lack of dashes! And also to Christy Aldridge at Grim Poppy Designs for her incredible talent and patience. If you like my cover (and I hope you do, because it's fabulous) you should check her out.

And now, my author friends…

The last time I released a book, I didn't have the professional support network I do now. I'm so glad that I found my tribe. THE COOL KIDS GROUP – you're all crazily talented, and I'm so proud to know you. THE SASSY SQUAD – Leigh Kenny and MJ Mars – you guys make me laugh and prevent nervous breakdowns every single day. Our group chat keeps me (relatively) sane. MY SLASHER QUEENS – Emerald O'Brien and Alan Shivers – thank you for being so generous with your time, and knowledge. You're incredible people.

The indie author community (particularly the horror authors). I've had the absolute pleasure to meet so many authors who are far more talented than I could ever hope to be, and who inspire me every day.

And, finally, to the readers who take a chance on indie authors. You guys are a special breed of people. You make smaller authors' lives infinitely better by existing. Every single person who has picked up one of my books, without judging the size of my following, or the fact that I'm self-published, I genuinely cannot thank you enough. Every single download, page read, purchase, and review, means more than you can ever imagine. I would be remiss not to mention the Books of Horror Facebook group. If you're not in that group, WHY? It's the best place for horror readers (and authors) on the internet. There's a misconception that horror lovers are dark, depressive types (and sometimes we are) but, for the most part, horror lovers are the kindest, loveliest people you could ever hope to meet (just don't feed them after midnight or get them wet).

## A little plea…

I hate to have to do this (it annoys me more than it annoys you, I promise) but, if you enjoyed this book , I would very much appreciate it if you could leave a review on Goodreads and/or Amazon. Reviews are the lifeblood of indie authors. They help us to reach a wider audience. It doesn't have to be anything fancy, even just a star-rating will do.  If you're not able to leave a review, but you still enjoyed the book, please tell the book-lovers in your life about it! Every little helps, and I am very grateful.

# CONNECT WITH SARAH JULES

You can find me across social media…

**Website:** www.sarahjuleswriting.com

**Facebook Page:** Sarah Jules Writing

**Instagram:** @sarahjuleswriting

**Goodreads:** Sarah Jules

**TikTok:** @sarahjulesauthor

# ABOUT SARAH JULES

Sarah Jules is an indie horror author from Yorkshire. She is a self-professed accidental hipster (who refuses to apologise for this). She is also the owner of Sarah Jules Writing Services, a job that allows her to work in her pyjamas, which she is immensely grateful for.

She currently has two previous releases, FOUND YOU & DON'T LIE.

If Sarah isn't working (or writing), you can find her with her nose stuck in a book, travelling the UK with her partner, and her rescue pup, or sweating it out in the gym. She is a mental health advocate, coffee-addict, and loves all things spooky and/or creepy.

Sarah blogs (super-hipster, she knows) about all things books, writing and publishing on both her Instagram (@sarahjuleswriting) and on her website www.sarahjuleswriting.com

# COMING SOON…

## BLOODY HELL

*AN ANTHOLOGY OF UK INDIE HORROR*

MJ Mars
M.L. Rayner
Ashley Lister
Jim Ody
Alexandra Nisneru
EC Samuels
Tom Carter
Philip Alexander Baker
CS Jones
JC Michael
Tim Stephens
David Watkins
Bethany Russo
Leigh Kenny
David K Slater
Dr Stuart Knott
Elizabeth J Brown
Jessica Huntley
Stephen Barnard
Marie Sinadjan
Mark MJ Green
Benjamin Langley
Brad Thomas
Elijah Frost
Lee Allen
William Long

**Edited by Sarah Jules**

**Illustrated by Rachael Rose**

***RELEASES AUGUST 1st, 2024***

# Extract from DON'T LIE

If you enjoyed *You Invited It In,* here's an extract from *DON'T LIE.*

## Chapter One

## *Quinn*

The pregnant rain cloud overhead looked fit to burst, an omen that I shouldn't have agreed to come on this stupid trip. Katie had been convincing, as she always was. 'One last blow out' before we all go our separate ways, that's what she said. And now here I was, in a glorified caravan, in the middle of nowhere. University had already ended. The metaphorical stage curtains drawing to a close, *exit stage left* and don't look back. There's this misconception that you can just walk into a job after university, and somebody will take you on, as long as you rid yourself of any moral fibre and accept whatever comes your way. I didn't want to be that person. I wouldn't be that person. I had a first-class honours degree, for God's sake. I'd passed my qualified teacher status with flying colours. There was no way I was going to go and work in a McDonald's, not after three years of stress up to my back teeth and very little sleep.

This is why I'd lied. How do you tell your only friends that everybody else on your course landed a teaching job except for you? Even the girls who cared more about over-drawing their lips and having eyelash in-fills every six weeks than imparting any education to the poor children in their teacher training classes had found schools willing to take them on. Schools that would force them through their NQT year and turn them into proper little professionals, but not me, and not for lack of trying. The only reason I'd agreed to come, other than Katie's pestering, was the fact that I needed a break from the constant stream of job applications. Have you ever filled out a teaching post application? It takes hours. What's wrong with sending off a CV and a personal statement? And so, I found myself unpacking my bag, listening to the people I'd lived with for the last three years, joking in the living room cum dining room cum kitchen, while I hung up my clothes in the children's wardrobe. We were only supposed to be here for three days, but old habits die hard. I couldn't live out of a suitcase.

I pulled out the Bio Oil from my toiletry bag, relieving it of its lid. Gripping the bottom of my t-shirt between my teeth, I rubbed the cool contents over my ribs; my chosen area for taking out my frustration. Scars, like jagged bite marks, decorated my skin. Bright white against my already painfully pale skin.

The door creaked open. I released my shirt from my mouth and straightened up to see Ellis leaning languidly in the doorway. I despised the way he made my skin prickle. The way I flushed. The way I forgot how to string a simple sentence together in his presence.

'There you are.' He smiled. If my life was an American teen sitcom, he'd be the jock. The one all the girls fawned over for his handsome jawline and naturally tanned skin. His smile could part the waves, fell the monster, cause the damsel in distress to swoon at his feet.

'Thought you'd vanished. We were just about to organise a search party,' he said when I failed to answer. The bottle of warm Budweiser was brought to his lips, my eyes fixed on his Adam's apple, bobbing up and down perilously. He was out-of-this-world beautiful and dear God, did he know it.

'I was just unpacking,' I explained, gesturing unnecessarily to the suitcase on the bed and the open wardrobe.

He shook his head at me, his eyes crinkling with the smile that tugged on his lips. He knew what I was like. Type A personality, he was always reminding me.

'I like your hair like that,' he said, stepping towards me. His fingers found my hair before I could back away. He'd been blowing hot and cold with me over the last couple of weeks, and I was determined not to act like a puppy dog, and instead respect myself a little, and demand respect in return.

'Thank you,' I said. My brunette hair was usually tied back in a ponytail somewhere near the base of my skull. But I'd decided to try something different. Instead, I allowed the natural curls to form as it dried, pulling hair from my temples back in plaits and securing them at the back of my head.

'Are you trying to impress someone? I hear Xan's single.' His lips were against mine before I could formulate a response. Gently, barely there. The kind of kiss that made me think there might be something real between us. Something that could last after we leave our student house and go into the big wide world to be real-life adults.

'Come on, Kate has dug out a set of cards and we're playing Ring of Fire.' Just like that, I came crashing back to earth. Ring of Fire. At nine o'clock in the morning, all because his ex suggested it. The future I, too often, imagined for the both of us dissolved into nothing as I traipsed along behind him, turning into the puppy dog I loathed to be, to play a drinking game. At 9 am. With my soon-to-be ex-housemates, all of whom had sorted their after-uni plans weeks ago. I had no job. No prospects. And my sort-of boyfriend was a huge man-child, who thought that drinking at 9 am was acceptable. My life had gone to shit.

# Chapter Two

## *Katie*

They walked back into the living room hand in hand, and it made blood rise to my temples. I could hear the rush of blood through my ears. I smiled, because that's what girls who are okay with their ex-boyfriend dating their roommate do. It wasn't that I wanted to be with him, necessarily. It was that I'd rather Quinn wasn't with him. I wrapped my hoody closer around my body. It was his. Ellis's. Not that Quinn knew that, but he did. I never gave it back after we broke up and the rules dictate that whatever items of clothing you *shared* with your ex before they became your ex become yours for life. Not only was it a power move to wear his jacket, but it just happened to be the perfect attire for a few days at *The Cabin.* That's what my parents called this place. A beautiful, double-wide lodge situated on a cliff edge on the east coast. It was beautiful, and the perfect place for what I had planned.

Leaning against the immaculate kitchen, complete with a state-of-the-art built-in fridge/freezer and stainless-steel fittings, Jude shuffled a deck of cards. His boyish frame made him look far younger than Xander and Ellis. He was constantly mistaken for a teenager and was always IDed whenever we went out for drinks, which was a lot. Or, it used to be a lot, before we all started to panic about the real life that was about to hit us smack bang in the face. This trip was our last big blow out. The last time we would all be together for the foreseeable future. We only had the house for another week before we were turfed out to be adults.

'So, Ring of Fire then?' I said chirpily. I had a role to fulfil. I'd invited them here, to The Cabin, it was my job to make sure they had a good time, initially at least. The whole trip, only three nights, had been planned out in advance and memorised down to the last detail.

'It's a bit early, isn't it?' Quinn said. She took a seat on the sofa across from me. Barely used. The satin taupe looked like it had never even been sat on, which wasn't far from the truth. The Cabin had been a last-ditch attempt to keep the family together before the façade was dropped and we all finally just admitted that we didn't like each other very much. Well, at all, really. If there had been a phone signal, other than that one spot at the crossroads before you turned off the main road and onto the dirt track that led to The Cabin, maybe we'd have managed. But it was a dead zone.

'Don't be a spoilsport,' Ellis said, sitting down beside her, even though there was a spot free next to me.

She stuck her tongue out at him childishly. I wanted to be sick. I caught Xander's eye, and he winked at me, showing me he noticed too, and that it irritated him as much as it did me. It felt nice to be supported. The trip had been partially Xander's idea anyway.

'How about we go to the beach instead?' Quinn suggested. Of course, she'd want to go to the beach. It was half-a-mile walk, across fields, and down cliffside steps that looked like something only Sherpas could negotiate. Plus, the weather was shit.

The plan didn't actually start until this afternoon, so what we did until then didn't really matter.

'Fine,' I said. 'Whatever. Let's go to the beach. You know there's nothing there though, right? It's just a beach and sand dunes.'

'And beer!' Ellis thrust his bottle into the air, slopping the contents onto the linoleum floor. He didn't notice.

'And beer,' Xander and Jude chorused, raising their own bottles. Until that moment, I hadn't even realised they'd opened their own drinks. They needed to stay sober (-ish) for this afternoon, or the plan wouldn't work.

I glared at Ellis, hoping my look said, *If you fuck this up for me, I will fucking kill you.* Metaphorically, of course. I'm not in the habit of killing ex-boyfriends, no matter how gorgeous (and irritating) they happened to be.

He held up his hands in a faux surrender, again slopping cheap lager onto the floor. I glanced down at it, hoping his line of sight would follow mine. It did.

'Sorry,' he mouthed to me, wiping the small puddle away with his socked foot.

'Let's go then. No point hanging around, is there?' I said, slipping my feet into my new white Converse, not the best idea for a trek across fields, but they were all I'd brought. The rest of the group followed suit. Ellis grabbed the crate of beer, and we were out of the door in less than a minute.

Allowing myself to fall behind, I watched as Xander and Jude chatted animatedly about some video game or anime I'd never heard of. Ellis and Quinn walked side by side, close enough that they'd be able to feel the electricity between one another, but not quite holding hands. I thought, and not for the first time, how weird our little group was. It was a coincidence that we'd landed in the same student house. Well, not Ellis and me. We'd filled out the forms so that we'd be placed together, but Quinn, Jude, and Xander were random additions.

It had been a risky decision to make, to board with your college boyfriend at university. For some people, the risk paid off. For us, it didn't, and I wound up living in the same house as my ex-boyfriend. And now he was dating the only other girl who lived there. What's the saying about not shitting where you eat? Well, we both did, and it worked out shittily for all involved. Ellis could have chosen any girl on campus to sleep around with, but he'd chosen Quinn. The girl who lived in the adjoining bedroom to me. If that wasn't payback for the years of bad karma I'd acquired, then I didn't know what was. All I knew was that I'd racked up enough bad karma to last a lifetime, so a little more wouldn't hurt.

# Chapter Three

## *Xander*

The beach was naff. Really fucking naff. In all fairness, Katie had warned me that The Cabin was in the shittiest of destinations, with the aim to encourage family bonding through the lack of any other decent amenities. At least it was deserted. We chose a spot in front of a sand dune, and each cracked open a bottle. Even Katie, who'd been preaching that we should all be sober for later, grabbed a drink. Perhaps she needed some Dutch courage. I couldn't blame her, not really. What we intended to do was fairly evil, really, but it was deserved. We'd been planning this trip for months and I thought it would feel thrilling for it to finally be here. Instead, it's a bit of a let-down. Like when you're a kid and you get all excited for Christmas Day and it winds up being just another day, except with a few extra pairs of socks you didn't want.

Katie and Quinn sat together slightly further away, laughing and joking. She played the part well, Katie, a doting best friend. You'd never know that she hated Quinn, not just from looking. You had to see past the frontage, to the reality beyond. The laugh that wasn't a true laugh. The forced happiness, forced conversation, forced enjoyment.

'You ready boys?' Ellis said, raising his beer in a mock salute.

'So ready,' I said. The grin on my face was real.

'For sure,' Jude said.

We all had our reasons for agreeing to Katie's little scheme. Some were more valid than others, but the outcome would be the same.

'We should go skinny dipping,' Katie said. My blood turned cold. This wasn't part of the plan. There was no way I'd be able to take my shirt off, in broad daylight, next to somebody who looked like Ellis. My limp, vampiric body, the type of somebody who spends too much time indoors, would only serve to make him look even more Greek-God-like.

'Are you trying to get me naked, Kate?' Ellis laughed. The two of them flirted in the most outrageous ways, and Quinn didn't seem to notice. Either that or pretending not to notice was some kind of self-preservation tactic. Not that he and Quinn were officially an item or anything. They were just sleeping together, or so he said. Why he'd be interested in somebody like Quinn, or even Katie for that matter, was completely beyond me. But, as usual, I laughed along, knowing my place in the hierarchy. I didn't have a vagina, and therefore I sat below the girls.

'Of course,' Katie said.

Quinn looked as pale as I felt. Just as I didn't want to compare my body to Ellis's, she wouldn't want her body compared to Katie's; the blonde bombshell with tits that held themselves up and an arse that should be on a Kardashian. Compared to Katie, Quinn looked like a boy. Given any chance, Katie would flaunt what she had in front of anybody willing to watch. Even in the late June drizzle, she wanted to get her tits out, go figure.

'Race you!' Ellis said, already throwing himself down the beach, losing items of clothing as he went. We hadn't brought towels, or a change of underwear. Ellis would pay for that later.

Katie shot after him, stripping to her bra and knickers and racing towards the frigid sea. Quinn shot me a worried look. I had no plans to move, and neither did Jude by the look of it. I shrugged at her. The ball was in her court.

I pulled out my phone, feigning indifference to the screeches coming from the water. The sounds confirmed that it was as cold as I suspected.

Holding up my phone in a way that I hoped looked like I was scrolling through Facebook, or Instagram, despite there being no internet access, I clicked on the camera app, zooming in to get a better look at the bodies in the water. My chest tightened at the sight of Ellis's chiselled chest. He jumped out of the water, splashing Katie. Click. The perfect shot. His body out of the water to mid-thigh. I zoomed in on the photo. It felt like every blood vessel within my body was on fire. Blood rushed down within my body and I shifted uncomfortably. There was even less chance of me following suit now.

Looking up, I noticed that Quinn had finally made up her mind and had sat down on the sand dune next to Jude. Exactly the response I'd expected from her. She pretended to play with her watch as she silently seethed about the fact that the guy she was madly in love with was playing with his ex-girlfriend, naked in the sea. You didn't have to be a mind reader to figure out that she was beyond annoyed.

Jude rolled his eyes at me. We both knew that she wouldn't say anything to Ellis. She didn't want to risk alienating him any further than she already had. The second she left the room, he forgot she existed. It was a sad sight to see, but something she wholeheartedly deserved. I hid my smile, focusing on Ellis, and wishing that it was me he was playing with, not Katie. The prospect of us wrestling amongst the white frothy waves was almost too much to bear. I took another sip of my beer and went over the plan of action. Everything had to be perfect if the prank, code-named GTB (or Get the Bitch) was going to work. This was the one chance for Quinn to face her comeuppance, to get what she deserved.

*Thank you for reading the extract of DON'T LIE. You can find the eBook on Amazon (and Kindle Unlimited) and the paperback is available from various websites.*

www.ingramcontent.com/pod-product-compliance
Lightning Source LLC
LaVergne TN
LVHW040820211224

799665LV00033B/282
*9781738487202*